CLAIMED BY HIM

NEW PLEASURES BOOK 1

M. S. PARKER

BELMONTE PUBLISHING, LLC

Copyright © 2018 Belmonte Publishing LLC

Published by Belmonte Publishing LLC

READING ORDER

Thank you so much for reading Claimed by Him, the first book in the New Pleasures series. If you'd like to read the complete series, I recommend reading them in this order:

ONE

HE WAS COMING.

My heart pounded as I ran through the darkened hallway. I could hear him behind me, and if he caught me, I'd die.

My hands were slick with blood, but I didn't think it was mine. My sides hurt from running, and my feet were cold, but I wasn't injured. Not yet. If he caught me though, I'd be worse than injured. I'd be dead.

Had he killed someone else? It certainly seemed possible.

I passed a mirror, and my reflection caught my eye. I missed a step. Something was wrong. I stopped and went over to examine myself in the mirror. This couldn't be me. I was a grown-up, but the girl in the looking glass wasn't a grown-up. She was tall, but not as tall as I knew I'd be someday. The ash blonde hair and china-blue eyes were the same, but the face was too round, too young. The hair too long.

If I knew I was older, did that mean he hadn't killed me?

"Get back here, you little brat!"

Ice flooded my veins. He was close, and he was angry.

He'd been angry for almost a year now. Every day, even if it was a good day, he found something to be angry about.

"Don't you go hiding now! That'll just make this worse!"

He was right. Hiding just made him madder, but I was scared of what he'd do if he found me. I'd been protected before, but never again.

I looked down at my hands, at the blood soaking my clothes. It was her blood. He'd hurt her. Killed her. She was gone, and no one would protect me anymore.

But I didn't need someone else to protect me. I was an adult. I could protect myself. Besides, this wasn't real. It was a dream.

The surrounding trees began to sway, bending low, reaching for me with their branches. I pushed them away, thin needles like razors that sliced my skin, mixing her blood with mine. I barely registered the pain. Pines. The smell of pines filled my nose. My chest tightened, and it was hard to breathe. I needed to get away.

I started running again, rocks cutting into my bare feet, bruising them, but I couldn't care about that. Not when I could hear him behind me, breaking things. I slammed the door behind me and then looked around, trying to find something I could put in front of it.

But it was glass. Even if I did manage to block it, he could just break through.

But I couldn't just wait here, unprotected either. I had to do something.

I spotted a rock. Not like a little stone or even some medium-sized flowerbed edging rock. This was huge. The kind of thing people put in their yards with their house numbers on them.

I went over to where it lay and put my hands on it. It was rough, like sandstone, but at least my hands wouldn't slip. The blood was tacky now, clinging to the rock as I braced my feet and pushed.

A blow shook the door, and my muscles screamed as I put more force into it. I needed to get this in front of the door. He was going to get inside. I couldn't make it easy for him.

Crying. Someone was crying.

An animal?

No, a kid. I was sure it was a kid.

He was screaming now. Not words. Just sound. So loud that people had to hear him.

No, wait, there were words. Bad words. Words that I wasn't allowed to repeat.

The rock didn't move, and the glass cracked. Fear dumped even more adrenaline into my body, and I could taste it in the back of my mouth. I was going to be sick.

I dropped to my knees and buried my face in my hands. The smell of blood filled my nose. It was sharp and metallic and made my stomach hurt.

I made a pained sound, and my eyes started watering.

This was more than just an upset stomach. It felt like fire was inside me, and I was being pulled apart. I retched, and it just made things worse. My head hurt, and I felt like I was going to pass out.

How could I pass out in a dream?

This had to be a dream. If it wasn't, it would be too horrible to consider.

The crying got worse. Why wouldn't someone shut him up? Why was he crying when I was the one hurting?

The glass cracked, and a dog started barking far away.

I screamed, and someone else screamed, and the dog barked, and the kid cried, and the door broke and—

I jerked awake, another scream dying in my throat. My heart was racing, my breathing ragged, and I leaned over to turn on the bedside light. Soft white light flooded the room, and I looked away to give my eyes a moment to adjust.

"Just a dream." I said the words out loud, as if that would make it all just magically disappear.

I shivered, the sweat on my body rapidly drying now that I was awake. My breathing and pulse were beginning to return to normal too. If this had been just a normal night-mare, I'd get up, maybe get some water, then climb back in bed.

I'd had these sorts of nightmares before.

Falling off a bridge. Spiders. Monkeys. Spider monkeys. Not actual spider monkeys but a creature that looked like a cross between a spider and a monkey.

Typical monsters that nightmares are made of.

This hadn't been one of those nightmares, the ones that were easy to shake off because they were ridiculous in the light of day, which meant that I wasn't going to be getting back to sleep anytime soon, if at all. I knew myself well enough to know that it'd be pointless to try.

I leaned back against my pillows and stared up at the ceil-ing. I needed to figure out what to do now. I had hours before I had to be anywhere, and I wouldn't be able to concentrate enough to read. I could've watched some TV, but the walls here were pretty thin, and I didn't want to bother anyone else. Besides, if I couldn't sleep, I could at least find some-thing worthwhile to do.

I got out of bed and turned on my overhead light before

turning off the lamp. I wasn't quite ready to be in the dark again. By the time I stepped outside, however, I was comfortable enough to appreciate the stars speckled across the rich, deep blue sky. I was too close to the city for it to be completely pitch black, so that helped too.

I'd already stretched, so once I hit the cool early morning air, I didn't have to stand around before jogging a few feet. I was just glad that it was May and not January.

I started off down the path, gradually moving from jogging to running. I wasn't doing a flat-out sprint, but I was moving at a pretty good clip when I turned onto the sidewalk and made my way deeper into the city.

Virginia and Indiana weren't really that similar in weather or terrain, but I had the strangest feeling of déjà vu as I ran. My nightmares – the really bad ones – did that to me sometimes. Made me feel like I was a kid again. It made sense that I'd feel that now. I'd loved to run as a kid too, and I'd been good at it. I'd actually done track in high school and made it to state a couple times.

One of the main reasons I'd always loved running was that it emptied my mind. I didn't have to think about anything but putting one foot in front of the other. Some people liked music when they ran, but I didn't. I preferred to hear what was going on around me. Birds. Traffic. People. Some of it was because I liked those sounds, but I knew that most of it was because I always wanted to be aware of my surroundings, even while my head was empty.

I'd made it a couple miles when I realized where I was. The hotel was nice enough, not too high end, but not too tacky either. It was perfect for businesses, especially ones who had guests staying for more than a few nights, and that was exactly why I'd ended up here, even if it hadn't been a conscious decision.

I headed inside without second-guessing myself. If I wasn't wanted, I'd go back, maybe go to the weight room until breakfast. But if I was wanted...well, that would be vastly more fun.

I waved at the man at the front desk, and he wiggled his fingers at me. I'd seen Hal a couple times over the last few weeks, and as long as he didn't get any complaints about me, he had no problem letting me walk right past. Unless someone high up found out about my clandestine visits, no one was going to say anything, and I didn't intend for anyone to find out. If it looked like that would happen, I had no problem walking away.

Right now, however, I intended to wipe my mind of everything that had been in it tonight. Give myself something better to think about. More enjoyable anyway.

I knocked on the door twice and then waited.

TWO

THE MAN WHO ANSWERED THE DOOR TO THE SUITE WAS thirty-three to my twenty-two years, but he was as fit as any field agent in his twenties. A fact that I could currently see since he wasn't wearing a shirt. I took a moment to appreciate the view, from his unruly dark brown hair to the blue-gray eyes that were still muddled with sleep, all the way down his chest to the trail of dark hair that disappeared under the waistband of his pants.

"Agent Kurth." I gave Clay a snappy little salute.

"Rona?" He rubbed the back of his neck as he looked behind him. "It's three in the morning."

I raised an eyebrow. "Are you going to invite me in?"

We didn't need to do the dance about why I was here so early. He'd known me for years, and he knew about my nightmares. He didn't know exactly what they were about since the subject had always been off-limits, but he knew they often resulted in insomnia.

When he showed back up in my life seven weeks ago, I'd

been glad to see him, but things hadn't become sexual until a few weeks later when I'd had the nightmare and gone for a run. Like tonight, I'd found myself outside his hotel room door, and one thing had led to another. We hadn't really talked about it since, but it'd become a thing between us, our friendship adding some 'benefits.' We could walk away at any time, opt out whenever we didn't feel like hooking up.

It was just sex between friends. That was all.

For a moment, I thought he was going to turn me away. It was early in the morning, after all, and he had to work early. We both did. Just because I couldn't sleep didn't mean he had to lose sleep too.

He didn't opt out though. He gestured for me to come in, then shut the door behind me.

"I wish you'd see someone about that nightmare," he said as he stepped past me and walked into the little kitchenette.

I kicked off my shoes and yanked down my pants, kicking them aside. "And I wish you'd stop talking and start working on distracting."

His eyes slid over my body, and heat followed his gaze. I hadn't worn anything sexy, but he never cared about that. It wasn't about what I was wearing, but what he was thinking about doing to me. I'd had a couple partners over the years, some of them bad, some good. Clay was better than good, *and* he was...inventive. It was a combination that kept me coming back for more, but not one that would get us past being friends who fucked.

"Come here."

When I reached him, he motioned toward the counter, and I lifted myself onto it. At two inches under six feet and with an athlete's build, I wasn't the sort of woman who got literally picked up by guys. I didn't mind though. I wasn't sure I'd ever met someone I trusted enough to let him manhandle me. If Clay didn't fit that particular qualification, I doubted anyone else would.

"Do you ever stop thinking?" Clay asked as he put his hands on my knees.

"What do you think?" I countered, wrapping my legs around his waist and pulling him closer.

Instead of answering, he captured my mouth in a deep, hot kiss, his tongue plundering, exploring. I ran my hands over his chest, his dark hair rough against my palms. He made a sound in the back of his throat when I rubbed my thumbs over his nipples. I used my nails then, blunt as they were, scraping them over the darker flesh, and he dug his fingers into my thighs.

"Damn, Rona," he groaned, tearing his mouth away from mine.

I flicked my tongue against one nipple, then the other. One hand moved under my shirt, and I stiffened for a moment, then relaxed, his signal that he could continue. We'd established boundaries the first time we were together. He could touch my breasts over my bra, but the shirt stayed on, and he didn't go anywhere else. I knew he'd felt some scar tissue a time or two, but he'd been careful to stay away from it.

And to never ask questions.

His free hand dropped between our bodies and his thumb pressed against the damp fabric between my legs. I made a low sound, my eyes closing. My head fell forward onto his shoulder, and I ran my hands up his back and then down to his ass. As his thumb pushed the material between my lips, he found that bundle of nerves and pressed against it. I slid my fingers under the waistband of his boxers, dipping my fingers into the two little dimples at the base of his spine.

Soft kisses trailed up my jawline, and then he took my earlobe between his teeth. Mouth and fingers worked together, stoking the fire low in my belly. For all our banter, when we finally got down to business, there was no waiting around, no dragging things out. This wasn't making love. It was having sex. Fucking. Physical pleasure and stress relief with a friend.

I squeezed my eyes closed, muscles tensing in anticipation of the relief that was only seconds away. He rubbed my clit harder, faster, and I came with a cry.

I turned my face into the place where his shoulder and neck met, panting. He gave me a moment to come down, and then he was taking a step back. I let him go, raising my head in time to see him drop his boxers. His cock was average length, but a little thicker than most, which meant it rubbed against a lot of nice places.

He fisted his cock as he opened a drawer and rummaged through it for a moment before pulling out a condom.

"You have them in every drawer here?" I laughed as the feeling returned to my legs. I could usually get myself off pretty well, but sometimes, it was nice to have someone else involved.

Clay shrugged and gave me that cocky grin of his. I'd masturbated to that smile plenty of times since I first met him, and it still turned me on. He was one of those pretty-boy sorts that people usually underestimated, but I'd always seen the intelligence in his eyes, and that just made him sexier in my opinion.

"Down," he ordered as he rolled on the condom.

I slid off the counter and took a moment to drop my panties before turning around and leaning over. I spread my legs and heard an appreciative sound from behind me.

"You have an amazing ass," he said as he ran his hands over both cheeks before dropping one hand down between my legs. "Damn, you're wet."

I nodded and braced myself on my forearms. He shoved two fingers inside me, and I let out a shaky breath. His fingers pumped in and out of me, twisting on every other thrust until he could add a third finger.

"Fuck!" I slapped the countertop. "Just get on with it!"

He chuckled and pulled his fingers out. "All right."

A moment later, he was pushing inside me, an inch at a time. I let out a long groan as my body stretched and molded itself around him. When he was finally inside, he reached under me and put his hands over my breasts, squeezing them for a moment before moving his hands back to my hips. He set a brutal pace, knowing that I'd tell him if he was being too rough. He hadn't gotten to that point yet. If anything, a part of me wished he'd push just a little bit further.

I wasn't going to complain though. Each snap of his hips sent a ripple of painful pleasure through me, driving me toward another orgasm, though it wouldn't come soon enough to catch him if I didn't help it along. Reaching underneath me, I pressed my fingers against my clit and made short, brisk circles – the best way to get me off after I'd already come once. Just as Clay's rhythm started faltering, I came again.

"Yes, yes, yes," I chanted as white-hot pleasure exploded through my body.

Clay was talking too, but I didn't pay much attention to

what he was saying. All I cared about was that the tension in my body had faded. I'd done what I'd come here to do.

After a couple seconds, he pulled out and moved away to take care of the condom. I rested a few moments longer and then straightened. I glanced at the clock. Dammit. Not enough time to attempt to go back to sleep.

I bent over to pick up my underwear and then went to the door for my pants. "I'm heading back," I called. He was in the bathroom, but I knew he could hear me.

"You want a ride?"

"No," I said. "I still have time to run back, shower, and get to class on time."

"I'll see you there then."

I heard the shower turn on as I pulled on my shoes. We both knew he only offered me a ride to be polite. No one at Quantico could know that Clay and I had been sleeping together. He wasn't my supervisor, but I doubted anyone would make that much of a distinction. I was eleven weeks into FBI training, and he was a guest lecturer. Not exactly kosher, even if we'd known each other before.

It didn't matter though. Once training was over, I'd be off to wherever I was assigned, and Clay would be off to the next lecture. We'd keep in touch, cross paths, maybe fuck. It'd never be anything more than that.

THREE

A QUICK BUT THOROUGH SHOWER AND A CUP OF COFFEE with a bagel were enough to wake me up completely. I might be flagging by the end of the day, but right now, I was good.

My first class would be with Clay, and it didn't matter how long he'd known me or the fact that we were sleeping together, he'd call on me if he thought I was dozing off. It was one of his favorite things to do to trainees.

It didn't matter if he was lecturing in a full auditorium or doing a more casual class in front of only a dozen people. He demanded attention. The thing that kept him from being a total asshole was that it was always about making sure people were learning what they needed to, so they'd do the best job possible. Sometimes, that meant embarrassing the hell out of someone. I sure as hell didn't want it to be me.

As I walked in the building, he was there. I barely glanced at him, but I felt his eyes on me as I walked past him and into the classroom. Today's lecture was about family annihilators and what made their psychopathy different from mass murderers or serial killers. We wouldn't be dealing with those sorts of cases much here in the FBI, but a family hostage taker could be an annihilator, and we'd need to know how to handle it differently than, say, someone who wanted something.

I couldn't say I was looking forward to it, but I'd deal with it the same way I'd dealt with everything else in my life. Besides, if I couldn't handle hearing about it, I'd be no good if I was called to a scene where it was the issue. As an Intelligence Analyst, that wouldn't be my usual case, but I believed in being prepared. Besides, there was no guarantee I'd actually make it in the field I'd chosen. Best to plan for all possible contingencies.

I usually sat in the first couple rows, but before I'd gone more than a few steps, the door opened behind me.

"Quick!"

I turned around, the movement automatic the moment I heard the familiar bark of Martin Edwards, one of the senior agents at Quantico. He wasn't the very top guy, but he was up there pretty far, and he scared the shit out of pretty much every trainee here. Not me, but I wasn't exactly the best judge when it came to fear. Not many people intimidated me. I couldn't think of a single one off the top of my head.

"Yes, sir?" I gave what I hoped was a polite but not too cheery smile.

He scowled at me, and my heart sank.

"Come with me."

Shit. Had someone figured out about Clay and me? Shit, *shit*! We could deny it, I supposed. The fact that we'd known each other before could be a believable reason for me visiting him at his hotel. He'd been my uncle's friend, after all.

When I was almost at the door, Agent Edwards walked away, and I hurried to keep up with him. He clearly didn't want to walk and talk, but I was fine with that. If he was about to chew me out for fooling around with Clay, I definitely didn't want to do it with an audience.

We made it all the way to his office without a single word being said, but as soon as he opened the door, he snapped at me, "Sit."

My stomach twisted. This was worse than I thought. I sat.

He settled in his chair and folded his hands in front of him. His face was back to being expressionless, but that didn't necessarily mean I was off the hook. Especially when he didn't start talking right away. I vaguely remembered hearing somewhere that he'd been one of the agency's top interrogators, and I finally admitted that I was in extremely deep shit.

"Rona Quick."

"Yes, sir?"

He gave me a look that said he hadn't wanted a response from me. He'd let me know if I was supposed to speak.

"Rona Elizabeth Quick." He reached forward and picked up a file folder from his desk. "That's the name you submitted on your application."

Fuck. It wasn't about Clay.

"Mother, Dana Quick. Father, unknown. Birthplace, Carmel, Indiana."

My pulse raced, but I didn't interrupt him as I tried to figure out exactly how bad this was going to be.

"Do I need to keep reading?" he asked, clearly expecting an answer this time.

"No, sir," I said quietly.

"You were asked if you were known by another name, and you said *no*. At the end of the application you were asked, as was every applicant, if the contents of the application were true to the best of your knowledge. You checked the 'I agree' box and signed underneath it. In doing so, you also accepted that lying on the form would be a federal offense."

I was going to be sick.

"We would normally have weeded out any discrepancies fairly early on, but you came with a letter of recommendation from one of our own—"

Shit. Clay.

"He didn't know," I whispered.

Edwards continued as if I hadn't even spoken. "Once we started looking, however, we found that you lied about several different things, including your name, your parentage, and the fact that a close family member had been convicted of a felony."

I'd known it was coming. If they'd found one lie, they'd found them all. They were all connected. Pick at a single thread long enough, and everything would unravel.

"I assume all of what we found is true, and not more fabrication."

I picked up the folder and glanced inside. I didn't need to read the details to know what it said. "It is."

"Did you really think that you could get away with it?" He seemed more curious now than angry.

I didn't want to look at him when I answered, but I forced myself to do exactly that. I'd known the risks and the consequences, and I'd made the decision anyway. "I didn't know, but I thought it was worth trying."

He tossed the folder back onto the desk. "Why didn't you fill it out truthfully?"

"I thought about it," I said, "but I knew if I did, it would all be there in my permanent file, where anyone could find it if they wanted to look hard enough."

"Your past wasn't *erased*, Miss Quick. It can still be found."

"You know all of it then." When he nodded, I continued, "I didn't want anyone thinking I had a weakness that could be exploited, that I wasn't strong enough to handle what someone might throw at me because of it. I didn't want instructors using it as a reason why I wouldn't make it. And I didn't want it to be all anyone saw when they looked at me."

Maybe the lengthy explanation wasn't really necessary, but I wanted it out there. I hadn't done it on a whim, or without understanding how serious it was. Other people might not get it – hell, I was pretty sure *no one* would get it – but I stood by my decision, even now.

Oh well. Nothing I could do about it now. Might as well get along with it.

"What happens now?" I asked.

"I need to know who knew about this," he said.

"No one."

He gave me a skeptical look.

"By the time I met Dr. Kurth, I'd already had my name legally changed," I said. "As for the rest of it, we didn't talk about it. Ever."

"And you believe that your uncle never told Agent Kurth anything?"

"He wouldn't have," I said. "Believe me, it was the last thing either of us ever wanted to talk about."

"What about when he talked to you about joining the agency?"

"I didn't say anything," I repeated. "He still doesn't know."

Edwards gave me a hard, searching look, and I suddenly understood what it must have been like to sit across from him in an interrogation room. As strong and stubborn as I usually considered myself, I couldn't imagine lasting very long against him.

"This isn't something that can be excused," he said, "no matter your reasoning. You have fifteen minutes to clean out your room and any other possessions you may have on the premises. Your clearance is revoked, and you'll be escorted from the grounds."

It could have been worse, I supposed. I could've ended up with a fine or jail time. Instead, I was only being kicked out of the FBI academy, bringing all of the plans I'd had for the future to a screeching halt. No Intelligence Analysis. No FBI. No solving cases or protecting people. From the first moment Clay had suggested the FBI to me, I'd been determined to make that my life.

I nodded, not trusting myself to speak. I waited until he called for someone to follow me to the dorms, and then hurried away, desperate to leave before anyone realized how humiliated I was. I heard Clay calling my name, but I refused to even look at him. It was better this way. Once he realized that I'd been lying to him for years, he wouldn't ever want to speak to me again, no matter our history.

Yet one more thing to add to the list of ways I'd fucked things up simply, so I wouldn't have to remember the past.

FOUR

Five Months Later

I KNEW THIS PLACE.

White curtains with teal trim, the 'grown-up' ones I'd wanted to replace the dinosaur ones I'd had since I was six. Dark gray carpeting that matched the rest of the rooms up here.

Right.

Stairs.

I was on the second floor. The scratch-scratch scratching was a tree branch against the aluminum siding. It was always louder after the leaves had fallen.

I frowned. What season was it? The room was warm enough, but it didn't feel artificial, and I didn't smell the almost antiseptic scent that came with filtered central air. I took a step toward the window, holding out my hand to see if I could feel a cold draft.

Nothing.

Not that it mattered whether it was spring, summer, fall, or winter. I was here, and it was good.

I breathed deeply, wanting to fix the smells in my mind. I knew this place, and it was important to me.

A sugar cookie candle mixed with vanilla body spray, but both faint, like neither of them had been used in a while. Carpet cleaner that was baking soda based. 'Sunshine-scented' laundry detergent or fabric softener came from the basket of clothes sitting at the base of the bed.

It was half-empty, like putting things away had been interrupted.

I'd been interrupted. This was my room. My home.

I'd been putting away my laundry when something caught my attention.

But what?

Fear was a metallic taste on the back of my tongue. Nothing here was scary, but my body was suddenly in fight-or-flight mode. A noise came from downstairs, and I took a step toward the door. I needed to go, but even as I thought it, I realized that I didn't want to go. I didn't want to know what was down there, waiting, lurking–

I jerked awake, my heart in my throat. For a moment, I didn't recognize my surroundings and the fear from the dream translated into real life. Then I saw Stevie, my stuffed blue whale, and knew I was home. Or at least where home had been for the past two months. Since I'd sold Anton's loft in New York before I'd gone to the academy, I didn't really have a home. I thought I'd be going straight from training to an assignment, and that's when I'd find a real place of my own. A place where I'd start a real life with a real home.

Instead, I'd gotten kicked out of the academy and found

myself homeless. I had money, at least, so I'd stayed in a hotel for a couple days as I figured out what I wanted to do. Then it'd been a weird game of darts where I'd moved from place to place, picking them at random by literally throwing a dart at a map on a dartboard.

I'd gone to Nashville, then Little Rock, then Sacramento, staying a couple weeks in each place while I tried to decide if there was anything there I actually wanted to do. I looked into a lot of different jobs, but I didn't find anything that really struck me.

I climbed out of bed and walked over to the window. The Rocky Mountains were about thirty to forty-five minutes from Fort Collins, Colorado, which meant that the west-facing window of my apartment had a gorgeous view.

I'd ended up here almost by accident. My dart throwing would've had me going to Denver, but that was one of the places I'd been hoping to be assigned. Instead, I'd picked a place at random, keeping it in the same area because I'd always wanted to see the Rockies. The moment I got here, I'd fallen in love.

Not with a person, of course. With the place. The more time I spent there, the more I loved it. I'd found an apartment, put down a deposit, and officially moved in by the end of August.

I moved away from the window and started my morning routine. It wasn't the same routine I'd had in college or at the academy, but it was a routine, and it worked for me. A mile run even though there was a bit of bite in the early October air, a shower, then work. Today, it went smoothly, and as I pulled my nearly shoulder-length hair back from my face, I'd mostly forgotten about the nightmare that had woken me up.

By the time I was ready to leave, I'd locked it all away, ready to focus on my day.

It was a quick commute to work since I lived next door, which I had a feeling I was going to love even more when the weather turned bad.

I had to admit, I thought my life had gone to shit after I was kicked out, but now I was starting to think that it might not have been such a bad thing after all. I wanted to help people, and I wasn't a fan of following the rules. What I was doing now fit around both of those things perfectly.

I smiled when I saw the sign on the door. *Burkart Investigations.* I'd been considering looking for a security job when I'd stumbled on this place, and it had felt more like coming home than anything else had in a long time. It wasn't just that the business side of things was exactly what I needed. It'd been Adare.

Speaking of the owner, she was sitting in her usual morning spot in the tiny lobby. She'd managed to squeeze four comfortable chairs into the space and still leave room for the coffee maker. Every morning, she'd choose one of the chairs and sit there with her coffee as she waited for the first client to come in.

"Morning," she said with a wan smile, looking more tired than usual.

"Good morning," I replied as I poured myself a cup and sat down across from her.

Adare Burkart was nearly fifty but looked closer to forty. She kept her jet-black hair pulled back in a simple ponytail and didn't even try to hide the streaks of silver. Of Middle Eastern ancestry, she had toffee-colored skin that never came close to burning in this high-altitude environment, unlike my own fair complexion.

My first assignment with her had been at the end of August, and I'd been tailing a man whose wife suspected was having an affair. Adare had warned me to use sunscreen, but I hadn't listened. I'd had on a hat, so my face hadn't been too bad, but by the end of the day, my arms had been painfully burned.

"You look tired," she said as she studied me over the rim of her mug. "I know you're not out partying until all hours, so what's keeping you from getting a good night's sleep?"

Adare lived in the apartment above the office, which meant she was my neighbor, but the buildings weren't quite close enough for her to hear me if I woke myself up screaming. I considered that a good thing. She'd been really good about not asking questions, especially for a private investigator, but she didn't let my desire for privacy keep her from checking on how I was doing.

"I haven't slept well the past couple nights," I admitted but didn't comment on the dark circles under her eyes and how sleep must be evading her too.

"Anything you want to talk about?"

Usually, when she asked that question, I said no, and we moved on, but today, I had something I could share. It wasn't the reason for last night's nightmare, but I knew it was the reason I'd been run-down in general the past few days. Besides, she deserved to know something about my past that went deeper than the surface.

"Three years ago, this past Friday, my uncle was murdered."

Adare's eyes widened, and I saw horror mixing with the

sympathy in her eyes. She didn't say anything though, letting me get through it at my own pace, revealing only what I wanted.

"Anton was an environmental lawyer in New York City, and we were close. October of my sophomore year at Columbia, a former client who wasn't happy with the way his case turned out showed up outside the courthouse. Gunshot to the heart. He bled out on the courthouse steps. The guy tried to kill himself too, but a cop stopped him. They got a full confession, and he's serving a life sentence, but it didn't change the fact that my uncle is gone."

After a moment of silence, Adare spoke, "I had a cousin who was killed in a hit and run when we were kids. They caught the woman the next street over when she ran her car up onto the sidewalk and into a lamppost. Her blood alcohol was three times the legal limit, and she'd lost her license for drunk driving three weeks before. She was convicted and sent to jail, but it didn't bring back my cousin."

She didn't explain why she shared the story, but I didn't need her to. I understood it completely. Just because we'd gotten justice, closure even, didn't make the hurt or anger any less. In a way that we wouldn't have wished on anyone, we understood each other.

Another few seconds passed before she broke the silence again, this time bringing attention back to work. "I've got an assignment for you."

I managed a partial smile. A distraction sounded good right about now.

FIVE

I'D ALWAYS HAD A DECENT SENSE OF DIRECTION, SO after being in Fort Collins for nearly two months, I knew my way around pretty well.

But I hadn't been to this particular area before. It was outside the central part of Fort Collins, but still part of the city. This was the place where the wealthiest inhabitants lived, including the Archers. After Adare told me that Jenna Archer had called to hire the firm, I'd taken a couple hours to do some basic research on the couple.

Damn.

Jenna Rose Lang Archer had hit the news four years ago when she'd gone on record as being a victim of childhood sexual abuse and an unwilling participant in more child pornography films than I even wanted to think about. There weren't a lot of details about her life or about the criminal proceedings that had led to the takedown of an unknown but vast number of people, but the interview she'd finally given two years after the fact had been enough for me to know she had overcome shit a hell of a lot more devastating than what I'd been through, and that was saying something.

The other thing I'd learned was that she'd married Rylan Archer, billionaire software designer and the owner of Archer Enterprises. For years, he'd been one of the most sought-after bachelors in the country. He and Jenna had been married for three years. I'd managed to find a single picture of their wedding, and it had been the official publicity shot they'd released themselves. I had a feeling that Jenna's computer skills had more to do with that than any scruples on the part of the media. The fact that there wasn't much in the way of links to any of the videos or pictures that had been taken of her as a kid told me that she'd done some serious computer magic. Not that I'd dug very deep. That wasn't my job.

I had no idea what my job was. Jenna hadn't told Adare, but the Archer name afforded some leeway when it came to things like this.

The address took me to an absolutely gorgeous house, the sort of place I'd be completely uncomfortable because I'd be worried about tracking dirt on the carpet.

When I knocked on the door, I half-expected a butler to answer, but it was a boy. Skinny, but in that way that kids had when they hit a growth spurt. He had a mop of dark, curly hair and a suspicious-looking scowl.

"What do you want?"

"Um, is your, um your...Mrs. Archer here?" I had to be at the wrong house. This kid was easily ten or so. Way too old to be the child of Jenna and Rylan Archer.

"Jenna!" he yelled over his shoulder but didn't move.

"You aren't supposed to be up." A woman's voice came

from behind him, and a moment later, she appeared.

She was shorter than me, with shoulder-length ebony hair, pale gray eyes, and one of those scary 'mom' faces even though I knew she was only a few years older than me. She wore jeans and a plain cotton shirt with three-quarter sleeves, neither of which were the sort of ragged chic that some rich people wore to try to convince themselves that they were down-to-earth. Her earrings were plain, and she wasn't wearing any makeup. This wasn't a woman who'd married into money and flaunted it.

"Get back to bed."

"I don't want to go to bed." The boy's tone was belligerent. "I'm not a little kid."

She didn't even blink. "You know the rules, Jeremiah. You stayed home from school. Unless I have to take you to the doctor, you have to stay in bed."

"I hate you." He stomped back into the house.

She held up a finger, listening for something. She must have heard it because she turned to me with a smile. "You're from Burkart Investigations?"

I held out my hand. "Rona Quick."

"Jenna Archer." She shook my hand, then stepped aside to let me in. "Come on in. Don't mind Jeremiah. He's been testing some boundaries lately."

"You have a beautiful home," I said as I followed her farther into the house.

"Thank you," she said.

We stopped in the kitchen, and she gestured to one of the chairs at the island in the center of the room. I sat down, and she went to the fridge.

"Can I get you something to drink?"

"No, thank you." I set my purse on the table and took out a notepad and pen.

She sat down across from me, a bottle of water between her hands. A glance down revealed a wicked looking scar on the inside of her left arm, nearly from wrist to elbow. When I looked back up, she was watching me.

"I tried to kill myself," she said matter-of-factly. "I was eight, and my life was fucked to hell." She shrugged. "It's better now."

I opened my mouth, then shut it. I was here to talk about whatever she'd hired the firm for, not her personal demons.

"Ask it," she said, the corner of her mouth quirking up. "It'll probably connect to why you're here in the first place."

"You have enough money to get the scar fixed even if insurance won't cover it," I pointed out.

"So why haven't I?" She finished my question.

I nodded.

"Valid question." She took a drink of water before answering. "I see my scars as proof that I survived some very hellish circumstances."

She brushed her fingers over her cheek where I noticed another scar, though this one was fainter. I probably wouldn't have even noticed it if she hadn't drawn attention to it.

"I like that," I said. I tugged at my shirt, suddenly feeling self-conscious. "I'll take some water, if the offer still stands."

"It does." She got another bottle of water and handed it to me. "How much do you know about me?"

"Basically, what a quick internet search could tell me," I said. "And I have a feeling you know exactly what that would turn up."

"I do." She gave me an approving nod. "Between the trial

and marrying Rylan, I knew people would be looking into me. I had to leave enough of the truth to satisfy most people."

I made an educated guess. "But I need to know more than that for whatever it is you want me to do."

"You do." Her smile faltered. "Will you be able to handle it? Listening to me tell you some pretty dark shit?"

In the back of my head, I heard the scratch-scratch scratching of a branch against aluminum siding.

"I can handle it."

"Then here it goes." She let out a slow breath and nodded. "My mom doesn't deserve to even be called a human, she was that horrible. She'd had an awful childhood too, but I can say with some authority that people can get beyond it and not treat their kids like shit."

I really hoped that was true.

"She was born Anna Newbury, but I knew her as Helen Kingston. She was twenty-three when I was born, but I wasn't her only kid. Just the only one she kept. As far as her official record shows, she had ten others. One died of SIDS, and the last one was stillborn. The rest went into the system." She went to take another drink and realized the bottle was empty. "I don't know why she kept me." She glanced at me, a bitter smile on her face. "I mean, I know why she *did* it. I just don't know why *I* was the one she picked. I've made my peace with it. More or less."

I hadn't been through the same things she had, but I could see a kindred spirit in her, someone I might actually be able to talk to who'd understand some of what I was going through. Maybe once this case was done, I could try it. Right now, I had to be professional.

"That's actually why I decided that it was time." She

suddenly looked nervous. "I'm at a good place now, about what I've been through, about who I am. I'd thought for a while that I'd found a healthy place, but after everything that happened four years ago, I knew I still had shit I had to deal with before Rylan and I even considered adopting."

Now the angry boy made sense. Him calling her by her first name. His age.

"We have a daughter too," she said with a smile. "Diana. She and Jeremiah are brother and sister. We didn't want to break them up. Not with everything they'd been through."

At that moment, I made a promise to myself that the next time I was feeling down about things I'd experienced, I'd remember this discussion to keep things in perspective.

"Anyway." She ran a hand through her hair and leaned back. "They're the reason I want to do it. If there's any way I can have a relationship with my brothers and sisters, I want it. And if they're the sort of people my kids can be around, I want them to have that too."

"You hired me to find your siblings?" I considered her for a moment, and then asked, "Why a PI rather than tracking them down online?"

"I spend enough time on the computer as it is," she said with a smile. "If I tried tracking them down like that, I'd get caught up, neglect things around here. If you get to a point where you need my help, I'll do it, but I want you to do the heavy lifting."

I nodded. "All right. I'd like to take some notes on what you know."

"No need," she said. "I've got everything I know printed out. It should give you some places to start."

And that was it. I had a new case to work.

SIX

I SPENT THE REST OF YESTERDAY GOING OVER ALL THE paperwork Jenna had given me, making notes and plans of action. This wouldn't be a one and done sort of case, and Jenna understood that. She'd reassured me that I could submit hours each week for payment, but that if another case came in, I could set hers aside. That was good, considering the enormity of what she was asking me to do.

Eight kids of varying ages, the oldest of whom Jenna believed was in his mid-thirties while the youngest would still be a child. Unknown birthdates as well as adoption dates, if they'd been adopted at all. Since the chances were that they'd been taken before they were more than a few years old, the chances of adoption were high, but not guaranteed. Unknown gender for the younger kids and only her mother's word regarding the gender of the older kids. Two birth states – the older ones in Florida and the younger in Wyoming.

Adare had let me have the big whiteboard so I could put

everything up to see it all at once, and I had a feeling that before this case was over, I was going to run out of space.

Once I'd organized everything, I was ready to begin. Since the case four years ago had been held here in Fort Collins, that was as good a place as any to start. Granted, that case had primarily been against Christophe Constantine, a pedophile who'd become obsessed with Jenna before the two of them had actually met, but he'd been connected to Helen Kingston.

With so many questions regarding where Anna Newbury had been born, when she changed her name, and what she'd been doing during the years prior to Jenna's birth, I needed to come at things from a different angle. Rather than starting at the beginning and working my way forward, I was going to start at the end.

Which was how I found myself entering hour number three in a dusty, mildew infested basement room at the Fort Collins courthouse.

I sneezed for what felt like the hundredth time and cursed under my breath. This was so unfair. Ninety-eight percent of the courthouse was modern, clean, and bright. The other two percent was the dingy corner where the things I wanted were being kept.

I put my hands on the small of my back and bent backward, giving a sigh of relief as my spine stretched. I didn't necessarily mind paperwork, but it wasn't my favorite thing in the world.

As I gave my eyes a bit of a break, I ran through what I'd learned so far.

Helen Kingston had been only one of Anna Newbury's many aliases. When it came to her 'work,' she'd gone by the name Helena King. In witness protection, her name had been Marcy Wakefield. After her arrest four years ago, her WITSEC identity had been compromised, so it had been included in the official record. She'd declined a new one, which meant that her name in the prison system had been Anna Newbury.

She'd also revealed a handful of other aliases. Crystal Troy. Ann Montgomery. Jasmine Sands. She'd used those names the times she'd been arrested for solicitation or drug possession in Florida. I doubted they were the only ones, but they would be a good place to start if her other names didn't turn up anything.

There was a good chance that I'd have to go to Florida to try to find Jenna's older siblings, but Helen / Ann had been put into her new life in Cheyenne, Wyoming, not that far from where we were now. It explained how she'd connected with Christophe, and how she'd gotten to Jenna before her handlers had known she skipped town. It was a good bet that the kids she'd had in WITSEC had been placed nearby and a much higher possibility that they were still in the same place compared to the older siblings.

I sneezed again and glared at the dusty files I'd been searching through. I'd come here assuming that I'd either be turned away, sent to the US Marshal service for answers, or shown to a computer where I could find court transcripts and allocutions. Instead, a rather perky paralegal had brought me down here with the explanation that the information I wanted was of such a sensitive nature that my access had to be restricted to solely what was available in hard copy.

Then she'd left me there. I'd heard her whistling as she made her way back to the stairs, the sound fading as she got farther away. I didn't know what other sorts of offices or storage rooms were down here, but in the past two hours, I hadn't seen or heard anyone else.

I made a mental note to make sure I left a good half hour before the building closed, or I could end up getting locked in. I doubted anyone checked down here very often.

I picked up my notepad and fanned my face. It might've been fall outside, but down here, it was sweltering. One would think that a basement would lean more toward the cooler end of the temperature range, and that was true in the hallway, but this particular room seemed to be situated right next to the boiler room...and had a connecting vent.

Between the heat and the dust, I was a mess by the time I finally packed it in. I'd gotten some good information, but I'd completely exhausted this particular source. After a shower, food, and some perspective, I'd sit down with my information and tweak my game plan for tomorrow.

All of those plans, however, went right out the window when I reached the top of my stairs. Leaning against the railing was a familiar figure with that same cocky grin that I both loved and hated.

I didn't even try to hide my surprise. "Clay? What are you doing here?"

He pushed himself off the railing, sticking his hands in his pockets as he moved to the side to let me through. "Isn't it obvious? I came for you."

I really hoped he didn't mean that like it sounded.

I doubted orange jumpsuits would be my best look.

SEVEN

WHEN HE DIDN'T AUTOMATICALLY START READING ME my rights, I took that as a good sign and opened the door.

"Come in," I said, hoping my voice didn't betray how nervous I felt. Just because he hadn't arrested me yet didn't mean he wasn't there because someone at the FBI had changed their mind about pressing charges.

"Nice place," Clay said as he followed me inside. "Much better than the dorms at Quantico."

I set down my papers and turned to give him a hard look. "Why are you here, Clay?" I held up a hand when he opened his mouth. I needed to clarify before he said something that made me want to smack him. "And don't tell me you came for me unless you want to explain exactly what you mean by that."

He looked puzzled, but not guilty, which I took as another good sign. I wasn't going to be completely at ease, though, until I heard the whole story.

"The last time I saw you, you were being escorted off

campus with all of your things. I tried contacting you, but you wouldn't respond. You disappeared without an explanation."

Now *I* was the one feeling guilty. "I got kicked out."

"Fuck," he said in a long, low voice. "What the hell, Rona?"

"How much did Anton tell you about our family? About why I was living with him?"

"He didn't. But I don't see the connection."

I sighed and rubbed my hand over my face. I didn't want to have this conversation. "If I tell you that I lied about something on my application, something from my past, but that I didn't want to talk about it, would you accept that?"

He closed the distance between us and took my hand, squeezing it. "You know you can tell me anything, right?"

I made myself meet his gaze, even as the emotion I saw there made me uncomfortable. "Not this. Not now."

I saw a flash of hurt, but it was gone almost faster than I registered it. He released my hand and wrapped his arms around me. "Okay then."

"Okay?"

He nodded, then bent his head and brushed his lips across mine. "Okay. No more questions. As long as you know you can come to me if you need to."

I didn't have the heart to tell him that I doubted I'd ever want to tell him what had happened in any more detail than I just had. I liked him, I really did, but it wasn't going to happen.

So I gave him the one thing I could.

Me.

I crashed my mouth into his, my teeth bruising against

my lips. I felt his surprise for a moment, and then he reacted the way he always had when we came together like this.

He palmed my ass, pulling me tighter against him. I pulled at his shirt, eager to feel his skin, to lose myself in him the way I had before. There'd probably end up being fallout when we were done, but right now, I didn't care. I hadn't let myself admit how much I'd missed him until now. We'd only slept together those couple months while we were in Virginia, but he'd been in and out of my life for years. Not enough to be a constant, but definitely enough for me to be able to count on him.

His mouth made its way down my jaw, his teeth scraping against my skin. His fingers moved across the skin at the top of my jeans before sliding under my shirt, fingers skimming the sliver of revealed flesh there. I thought for a moment that I'd have to remind him that the shirt stayed on, but then he turned me around and pulled me back against him. His cock was hard against my ass, and when he kissed the spot under my ear, a shiver ran through me.

I closed my eyes, letting my head fall to the side as he kissed his way down my neck. One arm stayed around my waist while he shoved his free hand down the front of my pants. I let out a yelp that turned into a whimper as his fingers plunged between my folds. I was barely damp, and the extra friction took my breath away. I gasped and squirmed, but he held me tight, forcing me toward climax with rough, abrupt strokes.

"Fuck, fuck, fuck, fuck," I panted, reaching behind me to grab at his leg. "Clay..."

His name ended in a cry as painful pleasure burst inside me, sending electricity racing across my nerves.

"There's one," he said with a smug smile. "Point the way to your bedroom, and we'll see how many more we can get."

<hr />

THE ANSWER TURNED out to be two more, for a total of three. I had to admit, there was something to be said for not being on a timetable.

"You've got a nice ceiling."

I turned to look at Clay. "What?"

"Your ceiling." He pointed. "It's nice."

I raised an eyebrow. "*That* is possibly the weirdest post-coital comment I've ever heard."

He reached over and pulled me to his side. It felt strange for a moment since we'd never really...*cuddled* before, but then the familiar scent and feel of him registered and I relaxed again.

"Would you prefer to talk about what happened? About why you never take your shirt off when we're together?" Clay's voice was strangely gentle. "There are a lot of other things we could talk about, but I meant what I said, Rona. I'm not going to push. I just don't want you to kick me out of bed right away."

I didn't look at him, but I shifted so that I could trace patterns on his bare chest. I had to make conversation, get his thoughts off what I was hiding. It shouldn't have been hard. It wasn't like Clay and I hadn't talked before. Even back at Quantico, after we'd started sleeping together, it hadn't been difficult to talk to him.

"Mind if I ask what you've been doing since I last saw

you?" Asking him about himself seemed like a good way to steer the conversation.

"I finished up my lecture series," he said, "and then I asked to be assigned somewhere as a field agent."

"Really?" I was genuinely surprised. "I thought you loved teaching."

He shrugged. "I did, and I might enjoy it again, but I wanted a change."

"To field work?"

"Working as a profiler isn't exactly the same as starting off as a junior agent," he pointed out. "Though I'm going the 'pair up and investigate' route rather than the 'sit in the office' route."

"You didn't get in any trouble over me, did you?"

He looked at me now, his fingers playing with the sleeve of my shirt. "No." His eyes widened. "Please tell me *that* wasn't why you left."

I shook my head. "As far as I know, they have no idea we were...you know."

He chuckled and kissed the top of my head. "Haven't you ever heard that if you can't say it, you shouldn't do it?"

I rolled my eyes, but I secretly enjoyed the fact that he was teasing me. It made the fact that we were laying here together seem less intense.

"Anyway, it took a while for things to go through since it's more of a specialized position, but I've been officially assigned to the Denver office for the past two weeks."

Denver. That was only a couple hours away.

"Did you request Denver?"

"No." He looked down at me again, expression serious

once more. "But I'd be lying if I said I didn't like the fact that you're not far away."

"Is that how you knew where I was?" I asked, keeping my tone light. "Inappropriate use of agency resources?" His cheeks turned red, and I couldn't stop myself from laughing. "Really, Clay?"

"That's not exactly how it was," he said. "The agency generally monitors trainees who have left the program, especially ones who..." The sentence trailed off, and he looked away.

"Who got kicked out," I finished for him.

He nodded. "All I did was ask Alphonso to keep me in the loop if your name popped up. He called me back at the beginning of last month to say that you'd applied for a PI license here in Fort Collins."

If Clay had just been some random hook up, it would've been creepy. Hell, if he'd been someone I'd been in a relationship with for two months, it would've been creepy. But after Anton died, he'd looked out for me. It was a completely Clay thing to do.

It could've been more than that, but I wasn't about to venture down *that* rabbit hole. I stuck with what was safe.

"How's work going?"

"Great," he said brightly. "I've been partnered with Raymond Matthews. He's a great agent, responsible for taking down dozens of child pornography and human trafficking rings in the past few years."

The name sounded familiar, but I couldn't quite place it. I filed it away to check in the future and focused my attention back on Clay and the new problem I'd just realized.

No timetable meant no specific time he had to leave. I'd

never had to think about how to ask a guy to leave before. Most of them couldn't wait to get away after we were finished, as if they were afraid I'd read more into it than sex. Or I'd been the one to leave before things became awkward.

I'd enjoyed the sex, and I was glad to see Clay again, but now I was wondering if it was such a good idea, making him think that we were going to pick up where we left off in Virginia. Or that we had something to pick up other than casual sex.

"I've got to head back," he said with a sigh.

"I understand." I tried not to sound too pleased with his statement. I really didn't want to risk my friendship with him, which meant I needed to figure out how to handle things before we did this again.

If we did this again.

EIGHT

I NEEDED TO TALK TO CLAY ABOUT WHERE THINGS between us stood, but it slipped to the back of my mind the next day as I took a trip to the Department of Child and Family Services. As a PI, I didn't have access to the sorts of warrants that I needed to get official information, but being a PI also meant that I didn't need to worry about making things follow the chain of evidence or be available for trial or anything like that. I needed leads, ideas, guidance. A paper trail would be nice, but it wasn't necessary.

Jenna nodded when I explained all of that to her, though I was sure she already knew it. She'd dealt enough with the legal system to understand the difference between what was true and what was legally usable.

"Did you do some breaking and entering?" She was smiling like it was all some joke, but I could see the flutter of anxiety in her eyes.

She was masking, and we both knew it, but I wasn't going to call her on it. I did my fair share of deflection and hiding, and knowing what little I did about her past, I didn't blame her a bit.

"I did not," I said with a smile. "But I did bring expensive coffee and donuts, which made a few people quite chatty. I can be charming when I want to be."

"I'm sure you can." She didn't look like she believed it for a moment. "Did it work, the donuts and coffee?"

"It did." I lifted a shoulder. "To some extent anyway."

"To some extent?"

I opened my notebook so I didn't get anything wrong and began with what I'd learned today.

"The woman known as Marcy Wakefield was what one caseworker called a 'frequent flyer.' Apparently, she liked telling people how she 'helped' couples who couldn't have kids, but any time they tried to get information from her about where those couples were, she blew them off."

"She told them she *helped*–" Jenna shut her mouth, pressing her lips together in a flat line. She gestured for me to go on.

"Are you sure you want to hear this?" I asked.

She nodded, her expression tight.

I continued, "Because they couldn't ever find anything under Marcy Wakefield, some of them thought she was lying to get attention, but a few others thought that she'd had kids under a different name. With this identity, she voluntarily gave up three children. One girl and twin boys. No one remembered exact ages, but their best guess was that the boys should be around ten or so. They don't have any record of a stillborn, but that wouldn't be something they'd keep track of anyway."

"Why was she allowed to keep having kids?" Jenna

shoved back from the table. As she paced, she kept talking, but I got the impression that she wasn't actually talking to me, but to herself. "I get the point of her body, her choice, but where's the line? When does it become about the kids' lives?" She looked at me, her pale eyes glittering with angry tears. "She had so many kids before she had me. It was all about protecting *her* rights, but what about mine? Who was looking out for me?"

I wasn't much of a hugger, and offering comfort wasn't one of my strengths, but I'd known enough injustice in my life to understand at least a fraction of what she was feeling right now. I stood and went over to her. I didn't feel comfortable hugging her – and I got the impression that she wouldn't have accepted a hug anyway – but I grabbed her hand and squeezed it. The fact that she let me hold it told me that she'd needed it more than she wanted to admit.

She closed her eyes and inhaled slowly, held it, then let out the air just as slowly. I waited in silence as she did it a half-dozen times and then opened her eyes.

"Sorry about that," she said, releasing my hand. "I thought I'd prepared myself for all the shit this was going to stir up, but I'd only been focusing on my anger at her. I didn't consider how angry I'd be at the system for letting it happen."

I knew some people might've argued that the system hadn't *let* it happen since it had intervened after obtaining the needed evidence, but I got what she meant. There was no such thing as a perfect justice system, and sometimes, it failed epically. Protecting the rights of individuals was important, but in this case, protecting one woman's rights had given her a victim to abuse for thirteen years.

"We don't have to keep going," I said. "I can do some

more work and pick up from here the next time. Give you a chance to prepare."

She shook her head. "No, I want to know everything you have. I won't say I'm okay, but I can handle it."

"All right."

We went back to our seats, and I found my place in my notes again.

"Theresa, the social worker who gave me the most information, hadn't actually worked on either of the cases. Her mentor, however, had dealt with the first case, so when the twins came in, the mentor had handled that case too, then debriefed with Theresa."

I'd actually been surprised at how willing to share Theresa had been, but I'd gotten the impression that more than a decade of dealing with some truly awful people had left her cynical and jaded. I knew not everyone who had Child Services involved in their lives was a criminal or abuser, but I was sure the negatives far outweighed the positives in this particular job.

"Obviously, she couldn't give me names, but she did say that the girl had been born when your moth..." I mentally cursed myself. "When Marcy / Helen... shit, how do people with multiple aliases deal with different names all the time?"

"Go ahead and call her Helen," Jenna said. "Or Marcy. It doesn't matter which name you use."

I nodded, understanding what Jenna wasn't saying. The name didn't matter, but she didn't want me referring to Helen as her mother. Not right now anyway. I couldn't blame her for that. I knew what it was like to not want to claim blood relations.

"Helen was pregnant when she was arrested in Florida.

Part of her witness protection deal was that she would sign the baby over to the state to be adopted. The Marshal service told her that it would be easier for her to settle into her new life that way, but that if no one adopted the baby in a year, they could talk about returning the child to her. Only a few days after she was born, the couple who'd taken her as a foster child applied to adopt her."

"Did they? Adopt her, I mean? I know sometimes people think they want a kid, but then the kid's too much to handle."

Although she didn't say it, I got the impression that she was speaking from experience. She'd been thirteen or so when she'd been put into the system, which was the same age I'd been when I'd gone to live with Anton. The social worker who'd come to talk to me and him had gone over some statistics when she thought I hadn't been listening. I couldn't remember the exact numbers, but the point she'd made was that babies got adopted, toddlers got adopted, but the older a kid became, the less likely their chances of finding a permanent home. A teenager like me...if Anton hadn't wanted to take me in, the likelihood that I would've been in and out of homes until I aged out was high.

"They did," I said. "She couldn't give details, but from what Theresa did tell me, they're a great family."

Jenna didn't try to hide the relief on her face. "And the boys?"

"They were with Helen for less than a year when she decided it was too much work. She'd considered keeping one and handing over the other, but the Marshal talked her into signing over both. They were in the system for less than a month before a family adopted both of them."

"They were kept together." Jenna's shoulders slumped a bit more, like another weight had been taken away.

"The last home visit went well," I added. "From everything Theresa told me, the three kids Helen had while in witness protection weren't abused or even neglected."

Jenna leaned forward and folded her arms on the table. She rested her head on them, face down so I couldn't see her expression. She didn't seem to be crying, but I didn't say anything. I was sure it was a lot to take in.

After a couple minutes of silence, she straightened. "Is that all?"

I shook my head. "There was one more thing. After Helen signed over the twins, the Marshal assigned to her came into Child and Family Services to speak with a supervisor. Theresa didn't know exactly what was said, but the gossip around the office was that he'd been asking about the possibility of petitioning the court to keep Helen from having any other children."

Jenna's eyes widened. "Seriously?"

"It's speculation," I reminded her. "But that is a distinct possibility."

I didn't add that if it was true, I was going to look into Helen's last pregnancy. My gut told me that if she knew she wouldn't be able to have any more kids, she could've been spiteful enough to have done something to the baby, especially since it was only three years later that she'd been arrested here in Fort Collins, when she went back to her old habits.

"That's a lot to take in," Jenna said, leaning back in her chair. "I'd known this wasn't going to be easy, but..." She shook her head. "Thank you."

"I'm just getting started," I promised her. "Unless you think it's too much."

"No," she said. "This is good. Knowing."

I put my notebook back into my purse and stood up. It wasn't even noon yet, but that was everything I had so far.

"Would you mind staying for a bit?" she asked. "I'm not quite ready to process everything on my own. Could we talk for a little while? Nothing heavy or important. Just stuff."

I probably wouldn't have done it for a random client, but I had a feeling that Jenna and I had already started venturing past client / PI territory and into friendship. I didn't have many friends, and certainly not women. She was someone I both liked and admired, someone I wanted to get to know better.

"Sure," I said, taking my seat again. "What do you want to talk about?"

"I don't know," she said with a laugh. "Something. Anything. Tell me something about yourself. Where are you from? Are you seeing someone? Did you do anything fun this week?"

I blurted out the first thing that popped into my head, "I saw an old friend a couple days ago."

"Oh?" She raised an eyebrow.

She was interested, but I could still see that shadow in her eyes. I understood the need for distraction instead of discussion, so I continued without any real prompting on her part.

"His name's Clay Kurth. He was a friend of my uncle's." The thought of Anton sent a familiar pang through me, but I didn't dwell on it. "He's kept an eye on me on and off over the years, but I haven't seen him in

49

months. He works for the FBI and was just transferred to Denver."

"A friend of your uncle's, who works for the FBI stopped by out of the clear blue in the middle of the week." Jenna got up and went over to the fridge. "And that's the first thing about this week that you thought to tell me? I'm no PI, but there's got to be more to the story than that."

Better to tell her about me and Clay's personal connection than my past, or my own connection to the FBI.

"Yeah, it's...complicated."

She brought over a bottle of water and set it in front of me. "Is it?"

I laughed and shook my head. "No, actually, you're right, it's not." I took a drink before continuing. "First, you need to know that my uncle wasn't like creepy old or anything, and Clay's younger than him. He's older than me, yeah, but it's not anything..."

"Inappropriate?" she suggested.

"Right," I agreed. "And we're not in a relationship or anything like that. Just friends...with certain benefits." The look Jenna gave me spoke volumes. "Believe me, neither of us are looking for anything else."

I was pretty sure that I hadn't convinced her, but she didn't press the matter.

"What does he do for the FBI?"

"He's a profiler, but I guess he's doing some field work now too. Partnered up with an agent named Raymond Matthews. I guess he's a big deal in the Denver office. Arrested a lot of bad guys."

A little crease appeared between Jenna's eyebrows, and I waited for her to tell me what was wrong, but she didn't.

"Are you doing anything tomorrow evening?"

I blinked at the change of subject and scrambled for an answer. "Um, nothing, as far as I know."

"Good," she said with a smile. "Come to dinner here at six. And bring your friend."

"Okay, I'll give him a call."

The words were out of my mouth before I really thought about them, and then I couldn't take them back. I'd have to call Clay and see if he wanted to come or deal with coming up with a decent lie. I didn't dislike the idea of spending time with him, but I knew things had to be handled carefully. I didn't want him getting the wrong idea and making things between us weird.

NINE

"Wow." CLAY STARED UP AT THE HOUSE, HIS EYES WIDE. "This is...impressive."

I chuckled and tugged on his shirtsleeve. "Come on. You keep ogling their house, and they're going to think you're a freak."

He grinned at me and reached for my hand. I let him take it because the front door was opening, and I didn't want him getting embarrassed if I pulled away. Besides, it was just holding my hand. It didn't have to *mean* anything.

Except the way he'd looked at me when he'd picked me up today told me that things were shifting between us, and I had a bad feeling that Jenna's comments regarding this relationship were going to be an issue now.

I didn't want to bring it up now though. We'd have a nice dinner, and I'd see where things went from there. If we had to have the talk, we'd have the talk then.

"Rona, it's nice to finally meet you."

Shit. Jenna's husband was *hot*.

I shook his hand, trying not to stare at him as I tried to figure out exactly what shade of blue-violet his eyes were. Then I realized that I was gaping at my friend's husband and flushed, turning to Jenna as Rylan introduced himself to Clay.

She grinned at me, her eyes laughing. Apparently, she knew the sort of effect he had on women. The moment he turned back to her, I knew why she didn't care about my unintentional ogling. He looked at her like she was the only person in the world. Like she *was* his world.

"Dad!" A little, dark-haired girl with big, shining eyes barreled down the stairs as we passed.

Rylan bent and picked her up. "Hey, Dee." He kissed her forehead. "Aren't you supposed to be upstairs taking a bath?"

She stuck out her bottom lip. "But I want to be down here with you and Mom."

"How about you go do what you're supposed to do, and I'll come up in a bit and read you a story?"

Her face lit up. "Okay."

"Now, say goodnight to everyone."

She looked at me, and then at Clay, tucking her face closer to Rylan's chest, suddenly shy. "Goodnight."

Clay and I smiled at her, and Rylan passed the little girl off to Jenna who gave her a hug and kiss. It wasn't until Diana turned to race back upstairs that I caught a glimpse of several round scars on her neck. I didn't have to be a doctor to know what those were.

Cigarette burns.

I felt sick. A glance toward Jenna had my eyes locking with hers. She gave me a short nod, her eyes burning with anger. Our interaction didn't last long, and when I turned my attention back to the guys, neither of them seemed to have noticed the exchange.

"Is Jeremiah feeling better?" I asked.

"Miraculous recovery," Rylan said wryly. "One day, he's so sick that he can't possibly go to school, but after spending an entire day in bed, eating nothing but crackers and soup, he's up and ready to go the next morning."

"Is Jeremiah your son?" Clay asked.

"He is," Jenna said. "Ten going on thirty."

"Thirty's old," Jeremiah said matter-of-factly as we entered the kitchen. "Can I be twenty-five instead?"

"Thirty's old?" Rylan asked. "Come on, kid, cut me some slack."

He shook his head and grinned. "Never."

Jenna ruffled his hair. "Thanks for cleaning up after you and Diana finished dinner."

Jeremiah ducked away from her hand, but he was still smiling. "You said I could play my new game if I did."

"Did you finish your homework?" Rylan asked.

"Yep," Jeremiah said proudly. "And I didn't need any help with it either."

"It's okay to ask for help if you need it," Jenna said, her smile softening. "But that's great that you understood everything."

"Does that mean I can go?"

"Two hours," Rylan said. "Then it's shower and bed."

He nodded and hurried away, not wanting to waste a single moment of his game playing time.

"We brought some wine." I held out the bottle. "I wasn't sure what kind, so I just grabbed one and crossed my fingers."

"I'll get some glasses," Jenna said as Rylan took the bottle.

"I wasn't sure if either of you had any food restrictions, so I went with variety. Salad, fruit salad, wedding soup, vegetarian lasagna, and baked chicken."

My jaw sagged. "That's a lot of food."

Rylan stopped next to her and put his hand on the small of her back before bending down to kiss the top of her head. "I told her we'd be eating leftovers for the next week, but she wanted to make sure we had something for everyone."

"We appreciate that," Clay said as he stepped up next to me, sliding his hand around my waist.

Shit. Touching me like we were a couple was bad enough but answering for both of us was what told me that I wouldn't be able to put off the discussion past tonight. Dinner, home, then talking.

I took a step forward, then reached for the salad bowl, like that was the entire reason I'd moved away from Clay. If I kept a little distance between us, things would be fine.

"I understand you work for the FBI," Jenna said as she poured us each a glass of wine.

"I'm a profiler, yes," Clay said as he accepted one of the glasses. "I used to be a guest lecturer at Quantico, but I recently decided I was ready for a change."

"Does that mean you lived in Virginia then?" Rylan asked. "How'd you end up in Fort Collins?"

"I'm actually in Denver," Clay explained.

Rylan's eyes slid from Clay to me and back again, but he didn't say anything else.

"Rona mentioned that you're paired with Raymond Matthews," Jenna said.

I raised an eyebrow. That seemed like an odd thing to have taken from our conversation yesterday.

"I am," Clay said, his expression curious. "Do you know him?"

"I do." Jenna glanced at me, a bit of color coming to her cheeks. "He and I have done some...work together. You'll probably hear my name from him at some point."

She'd done work with the FBI? It took me a moment, but then what I knew about Agent Matthews connected with what I knew about Jenna and the pieces fell into place. She helped him with his child pornography and human trafficking cases. Probably as a freelancer, or an off-the-books hacker.

For a moment, I wondered why she hadn't asked him to track down her siblings, but then remembered what I realized myself when I'd gone into Child Services. He was bound by a different set of rules than I was. At some point, we might need some help from someone with some power, but it was better to have me doing the work right now.

"How is Agent Matthews doing?" Rylan asked.

As Clay answered their questions, I helped set the table and hoped that he would come to the same conclusion as me. Otherwise, I was in for a very unpleasant night.

"I LIKE THEM," Clay said as we drove back to my apartment. "When I first saw that house, I wondered what in the world we were going to talk about, but they're really down to earth for people who have an insane amount of money."

"Probably because they weren't born to it," I said absently as I stared out the window. "Rylan made his own fortune as a software designer. Jenna wasn't rich before they got married, but she did have her own tech company."

"And now she works with the FBI as a consultant," he said, shaking his head. "Only you would find a way to work around being kicked out of the agency."

"I wasn't looking for a workaround," I said honestly. "I had no idea she had any connection beyond what had happened to her."

"What happened to her?"

I finally looked at him, surprised. "How could you have been in the FBI five years ago and *not* heard about Jenna Lang, especially with Agent Matthews as your partner?"

He frowned for a moment, then his eyes widened. "Shit. That was her?" He glanced at me. "You're not getting mixed up in all that, are you? That's not what she hired you to do?"

I shook my head. "I can't tell you what the case is, but I can tell you that it's not anything dangerous."

I didn't add that if Jenna ever asked me to help, I would. That wasn't his concern.

Which he would soon find out, because we were pulling up behind my building, and it was time to have the talk. When we got inside, he reached for me, and I took a step back. The surprise on his face confirmed that he and I weren't on the same page. The hurt said that I probably should've done this when I'd seen him in front of my door the first time.

"Rona?"

I sighed and sat down on the edge of the couch. "Sit, Clay. Please."

He did, but far enough from me that we wouldn't touch.

"We've had fun," I began, "but I told you when we first

started this, I wasn't looking for a relationship. You said you weren't either."

"I wasn't," he said quietly. "But what we have is good, Rona."

Shit. I really didn't want to do this, but I had to. No matter how much I liked him as a friend and enjoyed sex with him, I didn't want to be in a relationship with him. With anyone, actually. Maybe, one day, I'd change my mind, but I'd yet to find a man who made me want to consider it.

"It was," I agreed, "but we've gone back to having our own separate lives. You're in Denver, working a job that will probably have you spending long hours who knows where. I'm here, with my life. I don't want to lose your friendship, but if we try to keep what we have, where we are now, I think that's what's going to happen."

He wanted to argue, to try to talk me out of it. I could see it on his face.

"Please, Clay," I said. "It's for the best."

Finally, he nodded. "All right. Friends."

Relief flooded me. "Friends."

TEN

I took Sunday as a personal day. We weren't always open on weekends, but I'd never been the sort of person who did well relaxing in traditional ways. I'd taken the previous weekends as times to work on my laptop, to compile notes, the sorts of things I could do at home. I even spent time cleaning my entire apartment every other week.

Yesterday, however, I slept in, ate crap food, and did some reading. I was surprised by how much better I felt this morning. Sure, I'd gotten used to being around Clay when we were in Quantico, but I'd had five months to get used to not having him around. But I hadn't gotten closure until Saturday evening. Now, even though I knew I'd miss sex with him, I felt better knowing that I wasn't stringing him along.

This morning, I'd filled Adare in about where things had gone with Jenna's case, then she'd gone off to some appointment while I'd manned the office. She'd promised to bring back some super-caffeinated stuff for me to drink in exchange for me having to stay inside on a beautiful day.

When I heard the door to the office open, I didn't bother peeking outside, but rather called over my shoulder, "I hope you remembered the coffee. I got all of the paperwork done and all your files alphabetized."

"I apologize," a man's voice came from behind me, "I wasn't aware that coffee was required for a retainer."

I spun around, my foot catching on the back wheel of the chair. I stumbled, grabbing the edge of the desk to keep from falling. I didn't end up on the floor, but I did end up in a strange, awkward position when I finally raised my head.

And saw one of the most gorgeous men I'd ever seen. And considering how hot Rylan Archer and Clay were, that was saying something. Ruggedly handsome, he had just enough scruff to keep him from looking too polished. His hair was a rich brown color and tousled enough to tell me that the wind was kicking up outside. He was tall, well over six feet, and muscled enough to impress me. Then my eyes met his, and I almost stopped breathing. Pure, clear turquoise, like nothing I'd seen on a real person.

And he was definitely real.

And trying not to laugh at me.

"Are you, all right?" he asked as he walked into the office.

"Fine." I nodded and managed to straighten without looking like even more of a fool. "Sorry about that."

He shook his head. "No, no, it was completely my fault. I shouldn't have teased you. It's how I deal with stress. I'm sorry."

Stress. Right. He was here for a real reason, not to flirt with me. If he was even flirting with me in the first place. Which he wasn't. And I wasn't. Interested. I wasn't interested in him. Except as a client. That was all.

"Let's start over," he said. "I'm Jalen Larsen, and I came here to hire Burkart Investigations."

Starting over. That I could do. "I'm Rona Quick. Please have a seat, Mr. Larsen."

He didn't look much older than me, and from how he carried himself, I was willing to bet that he spent a lot of time having to prove to people that his age said nothing about his abilities.

"Tell me a little about what's wrong, and I'll tell you if I can help."

I gave him the same line that Adare always gave our clients. She'd warned me early on to never agree to take a case before hearing the details. We didn't turn people away because something was too difficult, but we did pick and choose our clients carefully. One of Adare's first clients had hired her to find his cheating, thieving wife. His words. Fortunately, Adare was thorough. It turned out that his wife had left him two months before because he'd been beating her the entire three years they'd been married.

"A business acquaintance of mine referred me to you," he began. "Rylan Archer. He said you were doing some work for his wife."

I folded my hands on the desk in front of me, careful to keep my expression neutral. Referrals were good, but I knew I had to be careful. He could have genuinely gotten a referral from Rylan, but he could also be lying. Rylan had money, and Jenna had been in the press. He could easily be a reporter fishing around for a story or even some lunatic trying to get at either one of them.

He gave me the sort of smile that told me he knew exactly

what I was thinking. He reached into his back pocket and pulled out a wallet.

"Here's my ID." He held out the thin piece of plastic. "Call Rylan and ask him if I'm legit. I just ask that you do it now. What I need is a bit time sensitive."

I took his ID, scrutinizing it for a moment before picking up my phone. If it was fake, it was the best one I'd ever seen. Still, I preferred to be cautious, especially considering what happened to Jenna a few years ago when an obsessed 'fan' had found her.

"Hello?" Rylan's voice came over the line.

"Rylan? It's Rona Quick. I have a referral in my office and just wanted to check with you that he was legit."

"If it's Jalen Larsen, then yes, I referred him to you. He's a good guy."

"Thanks." I breathed out a relieved sigh. "Tell Jenna I said hello."

"I will."

As I set down my phone, I handed Jalen back his ID. "What can I do for you, Mr. Larsen?"

"Jalen," he said, his long fingers wrapping around the card, "please."

He didn't seem like he was trying to flirt with me or use his first name to establish some sort of bond between us that would come back and bite me in the ass later, so I nodded.

When had I become such a cynic?

"One of my employees didn't show up for work this morning. He's been with me for four years, and he's never just not showed up. He's never even come in late. By the time he was a half-hour late, his supervisor came to me, concerned. We tried to get ahold of him, but I finally ended up going to his house. When he answered his door, I knew something was wrong."

I held up a finger, and Jalen paused. "His name?"

"Theo," he said. "Theo Ludwick."

I wrote the name down. "Go on."

"His daughter's missing." Jalen ran his hand over his face, rubbing his cheeks and chin like he wasn't used to having some stubble there. "Meka. She's fifteen and has been giving him trouble ever since her mom died."

"When was that?"

"Three years ago," he answered promptly. "Betsy had cancer. He was two weeks short of his one-year anniversary and didn't think he'd be able to take more than the three-day bereavement time. He'd already used up all of his other paid time taking care of her the last month before she died."

"Was he?"

Jalen's gaze jerked back to me. "Was he what?"

"Able to take the extra time?"

A muscle twitched in his jaw. "Of course. I'm a business-man, but I'm not more concerned with the bottom line than I am with doing the right thing."

A man with a strong moral code. I liked that. "I didn't mean to imply anything else. Just trying to get a feel for things."

He eyed me for a moment before continuing. "Meka's a freshman at Centennial High School. When she didn't come home Friday afternoon, he tried calling her, but all he got was her voicemail. He called the school and found out that she'd left after third period, giving the office a note that he'd supposedly written about visiting her mother's grave. He went to the cemetery, but she wasn't there, and the groundskeeper hadn't seen her."

"Has he filed a police report?" I asked.

His entire expression darkened as he scowled, the muscles in his jaw popping with agitation. "He went to the police Friday night and was told that she hadn't been gone long enough to file a missing person report. When he came back the next day, he was sent to talk to a random cop. He filed an official report, but the officer he spoke with said that Meka had most likely gone off with some friends for the weekend and she'd be back Sunday night, worried about getting in trouble."

I understood that having a waiting period to file a report cut down on cops wasting time looking for people who'd gone off to do something and forgot to leave a note, but there were times I thought that a lot more missing people would've been found unharmed if the search had begun right away. Just because a rebellious teenager ran away didn't mean she wasn't in danger.

"Theo spent all Saturday morning and afternoon trying to find her. He called friends, went on her social media accounts, even called her phone company to see if they had any way of tracking her phone."

Jalen's frustration was palpable, and I wondered if he was close to Theo and Meka, or if Jalen was simply the sort of person who cared that deeply. Rylan had vouched for him, and the way Rylan had been with Jenna and the kids the other night told me that he had high standards.

"According to the phone company, Meka's phone was off and showed no activity since Thursday night around nine o'clock. No one he spoke to could tell him anything."

I made a note to keep that in mind when speaking with Meka's classmates. Just because they hadn't talked to her dad didn't mean they were clueless. Friends would have wanted to keep her out of trouble, and enemies would've wanted to keep her missing longer, so she'd be in more trouble. Anyone who didn't think a fifteen-year-old girl would have those sorts of enemies was either naïve or had enjoyed a completely different experience growing up than I had.

"So, the police are actually looking for her?" I asked.

Jalen made a disgusted sound. "If you can call it that. As soon as Theo finished filling out the paperwork Saturday night, the cop tossed it onto a huge stack of other papers on a desk and said that the detective would take a look at it first thing. Theo called yesterday and was told that he'd be contacted when they had something. He wasn't given the detective's name or anything. No one came by the house or came to ask him questions. It seems like as soon as they heard she'd had some problems, they wrote her off as a runaway."

I frowned. I hadn't exactly spent much time working with the police department here, but Adare had told me that they were generally friendly and helpful. Then again, as far as I knew, she hadn't worked any missing kid cases.

"A couple questions," I said finally. "You know Mr. Ludwick well?"

"I do."

"Do you know of anyone who might want to hurt him? Get revenge on him?"

Jalen looked insulted that I'd even asked. "No! Of course not!"

I held up my hand. "I'm not trying to speak ill of him, but I need the truth. If he's gotten into any altercations that you know of, borrowed money, come into a lot of money recently."

Jalen shook his head. "Theo's a straight-shooter."

"You said that his wife died of cancer three years ago. Treatments can be extremely expensive."

"I covered them," Jalen said, the muscle in his jaw popping again. "My employees all have good health insurance, but I know that not everything gets covered. I have what I call 'grants' where if an employee or their immediate family have certain medical emergencies, they can apply to have some, or all of the costs covered."

I was impressed but pushed it aside. He wasn't the focus of the case.

"I'd like to take the case," I said, "but I need to be clear about something first. I don't care who's hiring me, who's paying for it. My goal is finding Meka and bringing her home safely. I'll probably step on some toes, ask things that people don't want me to ask, and they definitely don't want to answer."

"I'm okay with that," he said.

"I'm not a cop. I'm not collecting evidence to be used in court. That means no search warrants, but also that a good defense attorney would most likely get anything I find thrown out if there are charges to be brought. I'll ask questions, follow rumors. I don't need corroboration to follow a lead, and I don't need to read anyone their rights. I don't make arrests. It's all about finding Meka."

Jalen nodded. "If there are any legal issues, we'll take care of that later. Bringing Meka home is my top priority."

"Then we're on the same page." I held out my hand for him to shake. "I'll get one of our standard contracts, then take some contact information from you. I'll also want to come to your place of business tomorrow and talk to your employees. They probably don't have anything to do with this, but I want to be thorough."

"I appreciate that."

The moment he clasped my hand, electricity shot up my arm. I barely suppressed a shiver. Damn. If he wasn't a client, I'd be having a whole other conversation with him. As it was, I made a mental note to ask Adare the policy on hooking up with former clients.

A girl could dream, right?

ELEVEN

I was lost in the dark, and something was coming after me. That much was a fact. Why it was dark, I didn't know. It wasn't night. How I knew that particular bit of information, I didn't know, but it was the truth.

My eyes opened, but I still couldn't see. Had I been walking with my eyes closed? Was I still walking? I couldn't feel my legs moving. I couldn't feel them at all. I couldn't feel anything. Arms. Legs. Stomach. Head.

The realization should have frightened me, but it didn't. I existed, and that was enough for me.

Except I was being hunted.

I couldn't see it or hear it, but it was there, creeping, sneaking. It wanted to kill me. Cut me. Eat me. Destroy me.

The smell of cigarette smoke hit me all at once, making me gag and choke. It invaded my nose, my mouth. I tasted it on my tongue. My eyes burned, and I realized that I could feel some of my body again. I wished I couldn't. I hated the smoke more than I hated the dark.

A faint voice echoed in the distance. Someone was shouting, but I couldn't make out words. I felt the urgency, the desperation, but didn't know why. Were they being hunted too? Who were they? Could they see?

I wanted to tell them that I'd find them and help them, but I couldn't figure out how to get to them. Where were they? I shouted a question, but it disappeared even as the words left my mouth.

I tried again, putting more effort behind the attempt, but the words died again before they could take shape.

Was the thing hunting me also keeping me silent? Or was it keeping me from calling for help? Would I die here without being able to scream?

Was I in space? It made sense. No weight, no pressure, no light. But I could breathe. There wasn't any air in space. No stars. I wasn't in space.

Underwater? No, again, I could breathe.

Except...I didn't know if I was breathing. I couldn't feel my lungs expanding, couldn't feel the air entering my body. I tried holding my breath, but there wasn't anything to hold.

Was I dead? Had the thing in the dark caught me? Was this what dying and being dead was like? Hovering here in the darkness. Unable to do anything but think and fear and wonder what came next. I was still being hunted. Was death being hunted forever? If I was already dead, why did it matter if I was caught? Couldn't I give up and just let what happened happen? Would anyone even know if I gave up? Would they care?

Should I care? It would be so easy to surrender. To give in to the desire to not care. To give in to the darkness and just drift away into nothingness—

I woke with a gasp, awareness of air and body and pain and pulse and life rushing through me all at once, nearly overwhelming me. I fell back against my pillows and reached over to turn on my bedside light. I knew I wasn't in danger, that my apartment was safe, but it would take my body some time to catch up to logic. When it did, I'd get up and start getting ready for my day. Right now, I just kept repeating to myself that I was safe. No one was hunting me anymore.

I'D DONE my due diligence yesterday after Jalen left my office, pulling up as much information as I could find about Jalen, as well as Meka and Theo. The latter didn't have much in the way of a social media presence, but the other two had given me plenty to work with. Still, I was impressed as I entered the lobby of Sylph Industries.

"Good morning," Jalen said as he came toward me. "Thank you for coming in early. I appreciate how seriously you're taking this."

"I don't know yet if Meka ran away on her own, or if something happened to her, but the reasons don't matter to me as much as finding her does. Even if she made the decision to stay away, she's a minor and needs to be brought home."

I'd found enough on Theo to get the sense of him being a good man. I'd conduct my interview with him shortly, but my gut told me that he wasn't hurting his daughter. There was always a chance I was wrong, but I was as certain as I got without irrefutable proof in front of me.

"Thank you," Jalen repeated, taking my hand between both of his.

For a moment, I was caught by those incredible eyes, and everything else faded into the background. His hands were warm, and they sent a different sort of heat licking across my skin. My eyes dropped to his mouth for a brief moment, and I could almost feel his lips on mine. Would he taste as amazing as he smelled, I wondered.

Then he was stepping back, releasing my hands. He looked as shaky as I felt, but when he spoke, his voice was even and steady.

"Theo's already here," he said. "I put him in the chairs outside of my office three floors up. I figured you could use the space as you conduct interviews. We have a conference room on the second floor, but my office is a little more private. Unless, of course, you think it'd be better to be more visible."

I shook my head. "Good instincts. Have you told your other employees?"

"I wanted to talk to you about it before I made a decision either way. If you want them to know what's going on, I figured I'd tell them while you're talking to Theo."

If everyone was as accommodating as Jalen, I'd get through these interviews quick. "Tell them that they'll be asked some questions and that they need to be honest, but don't tell them what it's about. Often times, surprising someone with an unexpected question prompts a more honest reply than if someone is prepared for the subject matter."

Jalen nodded as we walked into the elevator. "I'll call for a meeting as soon as I show you to the office. Once you're done with Theo, how do you want everyone else called in?"

"You decide," I said. "You know better than I do the order of importance of various projects, as well as who's working on each team."

"All right."

The doors opened, and Jalen led me through a maze of cubicles and desks. A few of them had people already there, and they looked up as we passed. I saw curiosity on some of the faces, but all of them waved and smiled at Jalen. Instead of ignoring them to talk to me, he greeted each one by name. I wondered if he knew them because they were often here early, or if he knew all of his employees by name. The research I'd done indicated that the company wasn't vast, but it did employ a few dozen people, and wealthy CEOs were rarely hands-on.

A few comfortable-looking chairs sat in front of a door at the far side of the room, and a man sat in one. He had dark hair with a few bits of gray here and there, and an average build. His head was bent, keeping me from seeing his facial features and expression, but his posture spoke volumes. Anxiety rolled off him in waves, and he twisted his folded hands this way and that. When we were only a few feet away, he raised his head.

I would never claim to be a mind reader, but I liked to think I'd developed a good instinct for people, and if I was off, it was because I tended to be too cynical. I rarely believed the best in a person, especially if it was someone I hadn't known long enough to have established a pattern of behavior.

Despite Jalen's praise of Theo's character, I knew I had to be suspicious of him. Most violence in the world was committed by a person or persons who had a personal connection to the victim. The first suspect in a murder inves-

tigation was a spouse or significant other. The kidnapping of
a child was usually the result of a custody dispute or was
done by someone already in the child's life. I didn't like to
think of it, but it wasn't completely out of the realm of possibility for a parent to harm a child, then claim that they were
missing.

Theo got to his feet, rubbing his palms against his thighs.
He started to hold out a hand, but Jalen had already stepped
between us, reaching for the doorknob.

"Theo, this is Rona Quick, the private investigator I
hired." Jalen picked up a laptop from his desk. "Rona, you
can use my chair. I'll be out in an empty cubicle if either of
you need me."

I thanked him and moved around to the massive chair
behind the desk. As he passed Theo, he put his hand on the
other man's shoulder and squeezed.

"Answer everything she asks honestly and know that
she's just doing her job."

Theo nodded, rubbing his hands on his pants again
before folding them in his lap. As Jalen closed the door
behind him, Theo flinched at the sound, shifting in his chair.
His eyes darted all around the room, never resting in one
place too long.

He could be nervous, feeling guilty about something, or
the fidgeting could've been from lack of sleep and concern for
his daughter. The only way to get a feel for which was true
was to start talking to him and see what came out.

The starting point was simple. The follow-up questions
were where things got tough. I had to know what to ask, what
threads to pursue. "Tell me, in your own words, how things
unfolded."

With jerky, halting speech, he told me the same thing Jalen told me yesterday. A few of the details were different or new, but that made his story more credible. Anything that was too precise, too perfect, sounded memorized or coached. As a witness on the stand, a high level of unease might be due to the sheer terror of facing the defendant, or just the anxiety that came with testifying. Talking to me shouldn't have the same effect, especially for an adult with nothing to hide.

"And that's when Jalen, I mean, Mr. Larsen, came over to find out what was wrong." He finished his story, then fished something out of his pocket. A folded square of paper. "I wrote down the names of all of her friends and anyone else I could think of who might know where she is."

"Thank you." I took the paper and set it aside. "That will be very useful."

And not just to give me a place to start with Meka's social circles. A parent's knowledge about their child's friends was rarely one hundred percent accurate. The people he didn't know about would be even more important than the ones he did know.

"Just a reminder, Mr. Ludwick, that I am not a cop. I'm being paid to find your daughter and to bring her back safely. I don't make arrests, and the chances of me having to testify in court are slim. Anything I find would most likely not be usable in a legal situation. I don't have to get search warrants or read rights, but that also means that I am subject to the law myself. If I go into someone's house, I can be arrested for trespassing. Any risks I take are my choice, and I have no legal obligation to do anything I could get in trouble for. Also, people can lie to me without any criminal charges."

He nodded. "I just want her home safe." His face shone

with sincerity, and my suspicions of him dropped from fifty percent to twenty-five percent. Once I got a feel for how others viewed him, I'd re-evaluate.

"I need you to be honest about the answers you give me, even if you think it makes you or Meka look bad." When he nodded again, I went to my first question. "Has Meka been in any trouble recently? School or otherwise."

He didn't answer right away, appearing to think for a minute, which didn't necessarily mean he was lying or telling the truth. "I noticed she didn't seem to be bringing home much work, but when I asked her, she said that she was getting it done in school. When I called the school on Friday, they told me that they'd been trying to get ahold of me for two weeks to set up a meeting to talk about her not turning in homework and poor grades."

I made a note. "What about other kinds of trouble? Problems with the law? Outbursts at home?"

"No," he said hoarsely. He cleared his throat and continued, "I'm sure that cop I talked to would've told me if she'd gotten arrested or something."

As the interview progressed, I watched his body language as much as I listened to everything he said, from word choice to tone. He answered every question, clarifying when I asked for more, and never shirking from negatives. He painted a picture of a close father-daughter relationship bonded through mutual grief, then drifting apart as Meka became more withdrawn from him. He tried to balance understanding of sullen and rebellious behavior against being too permissive. Sometimes he succeeded, sometimes not.

By the time I finished with him, he looked even more exhausted than he already had. I couldn't imagine what he was going through, especially if he was as innocent as I believed.

"What do I do now?" he asked as he stood.

"If you can, go home. Try to sleep. Be there if she comes back. If you need to get out of the house, whether it's to work or just take a walk, make sure you have your cell phone with you, and leave a note in the house." I thought for a moment before adding, "And if the cops come to talk to you, whether or not you tell them about me is up to you. Technically, Jalen is the one who hired me, but as soon as I can completely clear you off the suspect list, he wants me to keep you up to speed on what I'm doing."

The acknowledgment that he was still currently on a suspect list didn't even phase him. This was a man who didn't care what anyone thought of him, as long as he had his daughter.

"I'll be in touch."

After he left, Jalen stuck his head in. "Do you want me to just send people in as you send others out or do you want to call them in yourself?"

I appreciated the fact that he asked, and that gratitude made me slip, and I smiled at him. "Send them in as other ones come out. These interviews will be much shorter than Mr. Ludwick's was."

Jalen nodded, then disappeared. A couple seconds later, a stern-looking brunette came into the office.

"Nanette Browne," she said, her tone softer than I would've guessed. "I'm the head of marketing."

I gave her my best professional smile, writing down her name and starting with the first question.

"How well do you know Theo Ludwick?"

EVEN THOUGH THE point of me talking to Jalen's employees was to get a feel for Theo and to see if anyone would have a reason to use his daughter against him, I couldn't help being impressed by the quality of the people I was meeting. They loved and respected Jalen, and they worked hard because they believed in him and in the work, they were doing. The work environment was professional but not overly authoritarian. He allowed room for fun and relaxation but didn't let it compromise the product.

But that wasn't the reason I was talking to every person in the company and asking them about Theo. I needed to focus on the case and put aside my own interest in my client.

Except nothing I heard today gave me any solid leads. Everyone agreed that Theo was a great guy. Honest, hardworking. They talked about how much he loved his daughter, how after his wife's death, she meant everything to him. None of them had ever seen him behave suspiciously, and none of them had ever seen him lose his temper, not even when he'd lost an entire day's worth of work when an intern spilled fruit juice on his laptop.

He was well-paid, but not excessively so. If someone wanted ransom, Meka wasn't necessarily the best target, unless they thought they could get Jalen to pay for her release. From what I knew about him, that wouldn't have actually been that far-fetched. Besides, that usually meant making contact to ask for ransom, and that hadn't happened.

I was still going to put everything on the board to make sure I hadn't missed anything, but I was as certain as I could be with what I had that neither Theo nor anyone he worked with was responsible for Meka's disappearance. Which meant I'd be taking a look at those names on Theo's list...and considering the fact that she might have run away.

TWELVE

ADARE HAD STOPPED BY LAST NIGHT AND TAKEN A LOOK at my whiteboard. I'd given her the basics of what I'd learned so far, and she agreed with me. Theo wasn't involved, and neither was anyone he worked with.

Which was why I was making my way to Centennial High School to see if I could scare some information out of teenagers. Okay, maybe not scare, but some kids needed a good kick in the ass before they did the right thing.

I wouldn't be using that particular pitch to get into the school.

Instead, I pasted on my best smile and lied through my teeth. I was Meka's aunt who'd moved out here to help get her back on track. To do that, I needed to talk to people who knew her. Fortunately, I was able to get Theo to call the school and let them know I was coming in, which meant that after I signed in and went through security, I was golden. I gave them Theo's list and asked them to send teachers and anyone else they thought of my way.

I was there for hours, talking to teachers and students, some of whom actually knew Meka, but others who'd only wanted to get out of class. Her teachers all said similar things about her. Bright girl. Lots of potential. Needed to focus more on school work than on socializing. She did moderately well on most of her tests, but she rarely did homework. She had a natural gift for math, so she did better there without the extra work.

All of those things could mean that something was wrong in her life, or it could just be that she was acting like a typical teenage girl.

Kids who were 'friendly' but weren't actual 'friends' described Meka as a loner, quiet, without many friends. But that wasn't how her friends thought of her. Three of the female names on Theo's list were friends, and they all said she was smart, funny, sarcastic, out-going. She was the one who tied them all together.

And then there were the boys.

According to them, Meka was both a slut and an ice princess. A prude. The sort of girl who'd give blowjobs to the entire football team one minute, and a cock-tease who never put out the next. She was described as trash who would spread her legs on the first date as well as one of those girls who wouldn't give any sort of action, no matter how much money a guy shelled out.

With all of it, good and bad, from friends or acquaintances or guys who wanted her, there was one thing that they all had in common.

A name.

Shawn Atkins.

Meka's boyfriend.

I didn't like him. He came into the room, sat down across from me, and I felt an immediate dislike for him. He was one of those smug guys who irked me to no end. He was older than Meka by a couple years, but the patchy scruff on his chin made me think he was trying to be even more 'mature.' He had messy blond hair that I was sure he thought made him look sexy or something, and dark eyes that were just as arrogant as the expression on his face. Not only arrogant but lecherous also.

The little bastard was checking me out.

"I hear you're Meka Ludwick's boyfriend."

"Boyfriend?" He snorted. "I don't tie myself down like that."

"Pretty much everyone says you're with her."

He looked up from ogling my chest and shrugged. "What can I say? Bitches dig me."

There was so much wrong with that sentence that I had to remind myself that this wasn't the time or the place to give him lessons on not being a misogynistic asshole.

"When was the last time you saw Meka?"

He shrugged again. "We hooked up the other night, but I ain't seen her since I left her, rode hard and put away wet, if you know what I mean."

"I'm going to ignore how little you know about women – and grammar – and stick to the matter at hand." I gave him a hard look. "Have you heard from her recently? Within the last couple days?"

He leaned forward, dropping his eyes to the front of my shirt again. "I thought you was here to help her with school shit. What's that got to do with the last time I talked to her?"

I sighed. This was the last person I had to talk to aside from the principal, and I'd lost my patience two 'players' ago.

"Yes or no. Just answer the question."

He shrugged. "My phone was broke all weekend."

I narrowed my eyes. A teenager who didn't get a new phone thirty seconds after their old one died was suspicious in my book. This kid was on my suspect list, but I needed to be careful to stay objective. Just because I thought he was an ass-hat didn't mean he had anything to do with Meka's disappearance. With teenage boys, natural teenage hormones and sociopathy were hard to tell apart.

"All right. If you hear from her, tell her to give her dad a call. He's worried." I watched him carefully, but that damn hair covered too much of his face for me to see even a flicker of guilt. "Get out of here."

I rubbed my temples as he left. I'd do my due diligence and talk to the principal, but I was ready to get out of there. I hadn't liked high school the first time through. Kids whispering rumors about why I didn't have parents. About why I changed in the bathroom instead of the locker room.

I shook my head and stood. The quicker I got it done, the quicker I could leave and organize my thoughts at home. Hopefully, I'd find something in all of my notes that would point me in the right direction.

I WALKED out of the school a few minutes after the last bell rang, and it amazed me how fast the hallways had cleared. The last of the buses were pulling out of the parking lot, and the kids who'd driven themselves were already long gone. I'd parked in the 'guest' lot which was right next to the teachers' lot, so my car wasn't the only one out there, but it still felt deserted.

I stopped next to my car, digging in my purse for my keys and mentally cursing myself for not having gotten them out while I was still inside. I caught a glimpse of a reflection in the driver's door window, and something about the looming figure told me that whoever was behind me didn't have honorable intentions.

I started to turn, my body automatically falling into the stance I'd learned in my self-defense classes years ago, but I wasn't fast enough. A fist collided with my jaw and pain exploded across my face. My lips smashed into my gums, and I tasted blood. My body jerked around, slamming against my car with bruising force. My vision went blurry, and I fought to keep from passing out. I didn't know what this guy wanted, but I didn't think for a moment that an unconscious me would have a better chance of making it out of this without any further injury.

"Nosy bitch," he growled as he grabbed my hair.

I let out a pained cry and grabbed at his arm. My nails slipped off the jacket he wore, the fabric too smooth to give me much purchase. Instead of holding me away from him, he trapped me between the door and his body, the weight of him preventing me from hitting or kicking him.

His face was masked, and all I could make out was that he was white and had brown eyes, neither of which was going to help when I called the cops on his ass. I let the anger bubble up inside me, burning away the slight edge of panic that wanted to come forward.

The fact that this behemoth of a man smelled like rotten cabbage helped. Nothing in my past was that gag inducing.

"Let go of me, you bastard," I said through gritted teeth.

"This is your only warning. Stop looking for the girl."

I barely had time to process the words before he slammed my head into the car. My knees buckled, and my arms dropped, giving him an open shot at my ribs. He hit me twice, forcing the air from my lungs, and then he let me fall to the blacktop.

I gasped, sucking in blood-flavored air that made me cough. Pain wracked my body, and I closed my eyes. I blocked out sight and sound, focused on the necessities. Air, for one. Breathing. Important.

One breath at a time. That was how I'd gotten through it before, how I'd been able to block out the agony to do what I needed to do. It took a minute, but I was finally able to get enough oxygen that my lungs weren't burning. It still hurt, but I was able to open my eyes. As I ignored the pain in my side, the throbbing in my jaw and head made themselves known but being able to breathe helped me push past it.

I braced my back on the car and pushed myself up until I was standing. The world spun for a moment, and I waited for it to pass. As soon as it did, I climbed into the car and drove away. I was halfway home before it even occurred to me that a hospital would possibly be a better idea. Then I realized that going to the hospital would mean calling the police, and I was no longer sure that was the best course of action. Whoever that man was, he'd proven that someone didn't want me to find Meka, and I doubted that a kid had that much pull. If I went to the cops, I could be putting her in more danger.

I knew enough basic first aid to know that I could patch myself up and keep an eye out for things like dizzy spells and nausea. I didn't want to go into a store like this, especially not now that I could feel blood oozing down the side of my face, but if I remembered correctly, the office had a first aid kit.

I dreaded trying to explain to Adare what happened, but when I walked into the office, she wasn't there. I saw a note on the desk telling me that she wasn't feeling great and had already gone upstairs. I made a mental note to check on her later, then started looking for the first aid kit.

I didn't realize that I hadn't locked the door behind me until I heard the door open. I spun around, a letter opener in hand, only to find Jalen standing there with a shocked look on his face.

"What the hell happened to you?"

THIRTEEN

I COULD'VE TAKEN HIS QUESTION AS AN INSULT, considering how intense he sounded, but the anger I saw on his face didn't support that particular theory. He was pissed that I was hurt. Not that *that* made much sense. He barely knew me.

"It's nothing," I said, turning back to the cabinet I was rummaging through. "Give me a moment."

"Sit down."

I turned to tell him I was okay and nearly collided with a broad, muscled chest. Damn. For a moment, I actually forgot what had happened and how much I hurt.

"I'm fine."

He reached out, his hand hovering over my injured cheek. The muscles in his jaw worked, those exquisite eyes of his flashing with a depth of emotion that surprised me.

"I'm assuming you have a good reason for not going to a hospital."

I started to nod, then winced at the pain in my head.

"They'll want to know what happened, and then they'll want to know why it happened. Considering how they've approached this case, I don't want to talk to them about it. It could put Meka in danger."

His expression darkened even more, and a little thrill went through me. "This was because of me?"

"It was a warning," I admitted. A stab of pain went through me, and I winced. As much as I loved being this close to him, I really wanted to get some painkillers and clean up a bit. "Can we have this discussion after I find the first aid kit?"

"Shit. I'm sorry."

I wasn't sure which was hotter, angry Jalen, or sheepish Jalen. I did know that I liked both of them a little too much.

"Sit," he said again, but his voice was gentler this time. "Where is it?"

I sank into Adare's seat. "I think it's in the bottom of the file cabinet over there. I haven't looked there yet."

I watched him as he walked across the room, and despite the pain I was in, I had to appreciate that tight ass of his. It was too bad he was completely off limits.

Completely.

"Found it." He came back in with a small metal box and then went into the bathroom for some wet paper towels.

Instead of handing them over so I could take care of myself, he stepped closer. His fingers held my chin in place as he dabbed at the cut over my eyebrow.

"How bad is it?"

"Not too bad," he said. "The bleedings already stopped, and I know how to make a butterfly bandage if there's not one in that kit already. Head wounds bleed a lot, even if they're shallow."

"Dealt with a lot of head injuries before?" I asked.

He gave me a wry smile. "I may have gotten into fights a time or two growing up." He gave a small chuckle before adding, "And fallen out of a tree more than once."

I laughed, then grimaced. "Bastard hit me in a jaw. Can you hand me one of those Vicodin? Adare left a couple in there from a few weeks back when she had a kidney stone."

Jalen's eyes narrowed, his anger back again. He grabbed the bottle and handed it to me. "Tell me what happened."

It wasn't a request this time, and a part of me wanted to refuse just to see what he'd do, but he was patching me up, so after I dry swallowed two of the pills, I gave him a quick but complete rundown of my last few hours.

"Fuck," he growled when I was finished. "I never would've...dammit!"

Tension radiated off him, but he still managed to put little butterfly bandages across the cut on my forehead. His fingers lightly traced over my cheek, the touch sending a sizzle of heat through me.

"Anything wrong with any of your teeth?" he asked, his expression serious. "Loose? Hurting? Cracked?"

"No, I think he didn't hit me as hard as he tried. I was turning my head when it happened."

He shook his head as he cupped my chin. His thumb slid across my bottom lip, careful not to press on the throbbing cut near the corner.

"Ribs?" he asked softly.

"Sore, but I don't think they're broken."

"That's good." He frowned. "I'm a little worried about your head though. You could have a concussion."

"I don't think so," I said, grinning at him. "I've gotten in more than one or two fights in my life. I know what to look out for."

He took a step back, dropping his hand. "Are you seriously smiling right now? You got beat up today."

"I didn't say it was fun." I stood, pressing my hand to my side as it protested. "But it comes with the job."

"You're a private investigator, not a cop," he pointed out with a little more vehemence than necessary.

"I appreciate the sentiment," I said, "and the doctoring, but stuff like this happens."

He shook his head. "Not anymore. Give me what you have, and I'll take it to the cops. You're done."

If he'd *asked* me if I wanted the police to take over, I might've considered it, but him telling me like that? *Hell* no.

"I'm not done." I squared my shoulders and glared up at him. "I promised Theo that I'd find his daughter, and I'm still going to do that."

"Like hell you are." He took a step toward me. "I'm the one who hired you, so I can fire you."

"Go ahead," I snapped back. "Fire me. Won't make a difference. I'm going to find her."

"Let the cops do their fucking job, Rona!" He was close enough now that I could again smell the soap he'd used to wash his hands. "You're through!"

"Do their job?!" The drugs were starting to work, and the anger under the pain was coming out now. "They don't give a damn about her! That's why you hired me in the first place!"

"I'll make them care," he said, his nostrils flaring in a way that shouldn't have been attractive but was. "I'm not going to let you get hurt like this again. It stops. Now."

I curbed my impulse to just kick him out of the office. "If

you want to take what I've found to the cops, that's your call, but I'm not done. I'll keep looking for her whether you're paying me or not."

He glared down at me. "You're infuriating! I'm just looking out for you."

"Yeah, well, I didn't ask you to."

He opened his mouth. Closed it. Then cursed.

And then he kissed me.

I was shocked enough that it took me a full three seconds to even realize that I was being kissed. Not because it was a bad kiss. It was the opposite, actually, something fierce and deep. Like he was trying to prove his point with sheer physical domination.

I grabbed the front of his shirt and pushed myself up on my toes, trying to take control of the kiss. For a moment, he let my tongue invade his mouth, let me *think* that I was in charge, and then his hands were on my hips, pulling me so tight against him that I could feel the hot, hard length of him pushing against my stomach.

His teeth sank into my bottom lip, and a flash of pain went through the sensitive flesh. I whimpered, and the sound seemed to break him from whatever had taken him over. He pulled his head back, air rasping in and out of his lungs, his eyes dark.

"Don't you dare stop," I said, shoving my hand between us. He groaned as I grabbed him through his pants. "You've got me all worked up here."

"You're hurt," he protested.

"I'm going to hurt *you* if you make me take care of things myself."

I wasn't sure if it was the threat, the image of me getting

myself off, or the fact that I was rubbing him harder than necessary, but something I did cut through any objections.

He grasped my hips and picked me up, turning us around so that he could set me on the desk. His mouth moved down my neck, and I let my head drop back. The Vicodin had left my mind floating, but not so much that I didn't know what I was doing or that I wanted to do it. With him. All the tension that had been between us just moments ago had shifted into a different sort of heat, and I knew that it might consume us both.

He grabbed the hem of my shirt, and I put my hands on his, pushing them down to the waistband of my pants before I reached for his zipper. I turned my head to take his mouth as I worked his pants open, but he immediately took control, his tongue tangling with mine.

I lifted my hips as he yanked down my pants, then I helped by kicking them off one leg. His teeth worried at my bottom lip as he pulled my panties to one side and pushed a finger inside me. I hissed, biting his lips, nails digging into his narrow hips, but I didn't even consider asking him to stop. If a single finger felt this good, I couldn't wait to feel what it was like to have him filling me.

I tugged on his pants, reaching around behind him to grab his ass with both hands. Fuck. It was just as tight as it looked. I pushed the pants lower until I could finally see that thick, hard shaft. Damn. He was big *all* over.

I cursed as he pulled his hand away from me, but then I realized that he was reaching into his back pocket. He tossed his wallet onto the top of the desk and retrieved a condom. I leaned forward and bit his chest through his shirt, earning a curse. His hands didn't even pause as he opened the packet and rolled the condom on, and I knew he wasn't going to take it easy on me unless I asked him to.

No way in hell was *that* going to happen.

He wrapped his fingers around the back of my neck, his thumb under the side of my jaw that wasn't throbbing. His eyes locked with mine, and I wrapped my legs around his waist. He held there for a moment, and when I didn't say anything, he eased the first inch inside me.

I breathed out a curse that turned into a muffled yell when he drove forward, filling me completely.

Concern etched his features. "Did I–?"

"No," I said quickly, breathless. "I'm good. Please, don't stop."

And that was the end of our conversation. I clung to him as he slammed into me, each stroke jarring my bruised ribs. Air burst from my lungs in pained breaths, but the ripples of pleasure that came from the friction of his body against mine helped even more than the Vicodin.

I squeezed my eyes closed, focusing on absorbing the conflicting sensations as I moved my body to meet his. There was no rhythm, no finesse, just friction and throbbing as all the right parts rubbed all the right ways, fit in all the right ways. I dropped one hand between us, fingers easily finding my throbbing clit.

We were both wound too tight to draw things out, and something like that would've made things far too intimate, so we both chased the end with little regard to anything else. As my orgasm hit me hard and fast, I gave myself over to it, grateful for the escape, however brief.

Jalen's mouth crashed into mine again, his kiss almost harsh as his body jerked, driving deep enough to make me gasp. A second orgasm followed the first. Or maybe it was the first getting stronger again. Either way, it sent pain and pleasure rocketing through my body, my pussy clamping down on his cock as he came with a grunt.

We stayed like that for several seconds, giving our bodies the opportunity to come down before we moved apart. Or, more accurately, he took a few steps back, then turned away. I stayed where I was, needing a few more moments for my battered body to recuperate. Neither one of us said anything, but it wasn't until he fixed his clothes and then headed for the door that I realized he didn't intend to say anything at all.

FOURTEEN

I DIDN'T BOTHER CLEANING MYSELF UP. INSTEAD, I quickly cleaned up the desk, picked up the bag of trash that now contained my bloody first aid stuff and a used condom, and then made my way next door to my apartment.

Until I was safely inside my place, I didn't acknowledge the anger that had been simmering inside me from the moment I'd come down from my high. But when I was finally in a place where I didn't have to worry about Adare coming in and asking questions, I let it all out.

"Fuck, fuck, fuck!" I tossed the trash bag into the kitchen trash and then leaned against the fridge. "What the *fuck* was I thinking?!"

I supposed most women would've been pissed at Jalen leaving without a word, but I knew I was the one who'd fucked up. It was beyond unprofessional, but I couldn't say that I'd never done that sort of thing before. Clay had been that sort of thing. Not illegal or immoral, really, but definitely not advisable.

I didn't do the casual sex thing very often, preferring instead to take care of things myself, but my last two partners had been questionable, I couldn't deny that. And I'd risked other people in both cases too. Clay had at least gone into things with his eyes open. He'd known that if we'd gotten caught, there'd be negative fallout to his career. Jalen wasn't the one who'd suffer consequences for what we'd done. If what had happened got out, the business could take a hit. Which meant Adare would take a hit. Not because she'd done something wrong, but because I'd been completely unprofessional.

Never again.

I stripped out of my clothes and tossed them into the hamper before going into the bathroom. While I showered, I made two important decisions.

One, I could never tell Adare what I'd done unless she asked. I wouldn't flat-out lie to her, but I didn't see any harm in keeping things quiet. If it became something important, I'd tell her, but otherwise, there wasn't a point.

Things might be awkward with Jalen – in fact, they almost definitely would be – but it wasn't like I actually had to work closely with him on the case. I could keep things completely professional until I found Meka. After that, our worlds would stay apart. We'd have no reason to see each other again.

When I climbed out of the shower, I felt physically cleaner, but that was about it. My body ached, and it wasn't all from the beating I'd taken. I could see marks on my neck and hips that I knew hadn't come from my assailant. A part of me wanted to put on long sleeves and pants, tear off the bandages that Jalen had put on the cut above my eyebrow, and remove any physical reminders of what happened.

But as I walked out of the bathroom, I knew that clothes and a new band-aid weren't going to make me forget any time soon. He'd been too big, too rough. Not because I hadn't wanted it that way. I had. And it had been amazing. If he hadn't been a client, I would've appreciated every ache and twinge that reminded me of how great it had been. Now, I only wanted to forget.

Well, I also wanted food.

I hadn't eaten much for lunch, and I'd burned far too many calories today not to get something in my system. I didn't, however, want to cook. I grabbed an individual cup serving of macaroni and cheese, followed the directions and then popped it into the microwave. While it cooked, I got out a bottle of water and told myself that alcohol was the last thing I needed, especially with the blows to the head I'd taken tonight.

I was just finishing my food when someone knocked on the door. I got up, wincing as things pulled and pushed. I should have thought to bring some of that Vicodin home with me. The over-the-counter stuff that I had here would barely take the edge off. If it was Adare on the other side of that door, it'd be worth telling her what happened just to ask her for something stronger.

The moment before I reached for the doorknob, I wondered if it was actually Jalen on the other side. If he'd come back to apologize for walking out, just leaving me there, sitting on the desk with my pants off, body bruised, pussy fucked. Or maybe he'd come back to yell at me. To tell me how unprofessional I'd been. That he'd been serious about firing me.

Except it wasn't Adare *or* Jalen standing there, staring at me in my bathrobe.

It was Clay.

"What happened to you?" Anger flashed in his eyes, but it wasn't like it had been with Jalen. At least on my end of things.

"Long story," I said, crossing my arms over my chest. "Why are you here?"

He scratched the back of his head. "Um...it's about your dad."

Well, shit.

Just when I thought today couldn't get any more fucked up.

FIFTEEN

I TRIED TO KEEP MY FACE BLANK AS I SAT DOWN, BUT Clay knew me too well.

"Okay, seriously, what happened to you?"

"I got mugged," I said. "Nothing broken, and nothing some rest and painkillers can't handle."

He sighed as he sat down next to me. "You know I can tell when you're lying, right?"

"I'm not lying."

He raised an eyebrow. "You're not?"

I deflected. "Is this really the discussion we need to be having now? You said you wanted to talk to me about my dad. How...what..."

I didn't know what question to ask even though my brain had been scrambling to think of something.

"I know," Clay said quietly. "I know everything. I saw the file."

The air rushed right out of my lungs. When he said he

needed to talk about my dad, I'd thought that maybe he'd heard a rumor that he wanted to discuss. But this...this was more than I'd thought it would be.

"I can explain," I said. "Anton didn't tell you because we didn't like talking about it."

Clay shook his head. "That's not it. I understand why neither of you wanted to talk about it." He put his hand on my knee for a moment, but there was nothing sexual about it. "I'm so sorry."

I nodded, then took a slow breath. "What do you want to know?" I didn't want to talk about it now any more than I had before, but he knew enough that it'd be better to give him answers than let him guess.

"I'm not here for answers either." He still looked sympathetic, but it moved to the background. He was all business now. "Your father filed an appeal."

I felt the blood drain from my face as I shook my head. "That's not possible. The case was airtight."

"Because of your testimony," Clay said. "And there wasn't anything wrong with that. He's claiming insufficient counsel."

"Bullshit," I said.

"Yeah, that's what pretty much everyone involved in the case thinks." He stood and went into the kitchen, coming back a few seconds later with two bottles of water. "I'd say you need alcohol for this conversation, but it's not a good idea to mix it with whatever you're taking for that." He gestured at my face.

"Thanks," I said dryly. "You sure know how to make a girl feel special."

He sat back down next to me but put a little more space

between us this time. I knew this was serious, but a part of me wanted to keep going with the easy banter the two of us had always enjoyed, even back when I was just Anton's little sister. Once he started giving me details, I couldn't pretend it wasn't happening.

"The defense attorney who handled your father's case was arrested three weeks ago on bribery charges."

"Shit."

Clay nodded. "Exactly."

"All of that lawyer's cases are getting reviewed then?" I asked. "As a precaution?"

"I wish it was that simple." He took a drink before continuing. "Every defendant he ever worked for is filing an appeal, but not all of them will be granted a new trial. They have to prove that something happened in their case."

"That's what, hundreds of cases? It'll be years before anything happens, right? And with my testimony, there's no way he could be granted a new trial. I was there. I told everything that happened." Panic clawed its way up my throat.

"Your dad's case is one of the ones that was specifically involved in the investigation that busted his lawyer," Clay said. "It was a corruption case, internal affairs looking into some cops they thought were dirty. One of them got arrested and started talking, implicating a handful of other cops – some officers and some detectives – as well as a couple other lawyers."

"What's the connection?" I spoke around the lump in my throat.

"One of the detectives implicated was the same one who took your witness statement back then, and the officer who gave the name was one of the first responders. Both men's financials show payments from the defense attorney to their personal accounts around the time of your father's trial. They both gave sworn statements that they'd been paid to make sure your father went to jail."

"And since the bribes were for a conviction rather than an acquittal, my dad's appealing on the grounds that his defense attorney was actually working against him." I followed the facts to their obvious conclusion.

"Two days ago, Internal Affairs found the payments. They were verified and submitted as evidence in your father's appeal. This morning, the judge granted him a new trial."

Even though I'd been expecting this outcome from the moment Clay had started explaining things, it still felt like I'd gotten hit again. My chest tightened, and my lungs constricted, making it difficult to breathe. With everything that had happened today, I wasn't sure I could take anything else, but I couldn't show that side of myself to Clay. Not when we needed to keep some space between us.

"They're going to need you to testify."

I nodded, unable to speak just yet. That wasn't a surprise either. There had been other people involved, other victims, but nothing had been more damning than his thirteen-year-old daughter sitting in the witness stand and talking about what he'd done. I'd been old enough and strong enough to stand up to the defense attorney's questions, but young enough that it had been difficult to find a way to discredit me without getting a sympathy vote from the jury.

"I know it's been nine years, but—"

"It's not something you forget," I interrupted quietly. "I remember every detail."

He touched me now, taking my hand and holding it between his. "I wish I could tell you that you wouldn't need to do this, but it's out of my hands."

"It's all right," I lied.

"No, it's not."

I managed a partial smile. "No, it's not," I agreed. "But I survived it then, and I'll survive it now."

"You had Anton then," Clay said, squeezing my hand. "And you'll have me this time. I already put in a formal request to be involved with making sure you're protected and that you get where you need to go."

"You didn't have to do that," I protested.

"You're my friend," he said simply. "And it's what Anton would've wanted me to do."

I nodded because I didn't have it in me to argue. My choices were simple. Testify and relive that awful day, knowing that some suit was going to pick apart every single thing I said and try to make me out to be unreliable. Or option two, refuse to testify and watch as my father went free.

No way in hell was I going to let that monster out.

"I can stay for a while," Clay said, "so you aren't alone. No funny business, I promise."

"Do you have a room reserved somewhere?"

"I was planning on driving back tonight."

"No," I said, removing my hand from his. "You're staying on the couch." I pointed at him. "And no arguing."

He held up his hands in surrender, and I went to find bedding for the couch. Saying that I didn't want him driving back tonight was true, but it also gave him an excuse to stay and keep an eye on me.

As much as it pained me to admit it, it also meant I didn't

have to be alone tonight, and we could keep pretending that things between us were the same as they were before we'd started sleeping together.

I needed that right now because things were going to get worse before they got better.

SIXTEEN

I COULDN'T BREATHE. EVERY BREATH I TRIED TO TAKE WAS agony, jarring out what little air I managed to take in. My lungs burned, fire spreading across seared nerves down to my fingers and my toes so that every inch of me was in anguish.

My teeth clacked together as I shivered, each tremor sending another convulsion of pain through me. I was cold, and I was burning. Every gasp was a cry, a whimper. My cheeks were wet, but I couldn't tell if the liquid was tears or blood.

I could smell blood. That sharp, metallic scent that always made me nauseous surrounded me. I didn't want to open my eyes, because then I'd see it all around me. I'd see where I was bleeding. See that I was dying.

Because I had to be dying. It was the only possible explanation. The only explanation I would accept. Because if I wasn't dying, that meant I'd have to endure this and I couldn't. I needed it to be over. I couldn't take it. I wasn't strong enough.

I wasn't.

I wasn't.

But I had to be.

Because I heard screaming. Screaming and blood and death and pain and all of it forever and–

I slapped my hand over my mouth as I jerked awake, barely managing to hold in a scream. I pressed my lips tightly together as I tried to talk myself down.

It wasn't real. Not anymore. It hadn't happened again. I was in pain from some asshole beating me up. It wasn't fun, but it wasn't anything to be scared of. Not like what had happened before. I was safe here. I was home. This was a safe neighborhood. A safe building.

And I wasn't alone. Clay was here with me. He was just a few feet away, out in the living room. He wouldn't let anything bad happen to me. No one would get to me here. I was safe.

That was what I needed to remember. That I was safe.

I MANAGED a couple short naps before I finally gave up trying to actually sleep. Not wanting to bother Clay, I didn't turn on any lights as I made my way to the bathroom. I had to admit, I'd had my doubts about this place when Adare had first suggested that I rent it. I'd been a little spoiled by the loft Anton had left me in Hell's Kitchen, but once I'd settled in here, I'd realized how good I'd gotten it. No obnoxious neighbors. And no one complaining that I'd used up all the hot water.

When I finally came out of the bathroom, I felt a lot more

human and a little bit less sore. The hot water had eased the aches in my muscles, and while moving around wasn't going to be the most fun thing in the world, I knew if I rested too much, I'd get stiff, and it'd be worse in the long run.

I'd put a new band-aid on my forehead, which looked better, but the bruises on the side of my face looked worse. I'd try later to cover them with makeup, but for right now, it was just me and Clay, and he'd already seen them.

"Your couch sucks," Clay grumbled as he staggered past me. His hair stuck up at all angles and the pattern of fabric on the couch had imprinted itself on his face.

"Towels are in the cabinet next to the sink," I called after him. "I'll make us some breakfast before you hit the road."

"That would be great." His voice was muffled by the door. "When do you have to be at work?"

"Adare lets me come and go at my own time," I said. "It all depends on the case."

I frowned. My case. With Clay's sudden appearance and the announcement about my father's new trial, I'd almost forgotten about Meka. Even after the assault, I'd planned on looking over my notes and figuring out my next move.

Then Jalen happened.

Then Clay.

The shower was on again, which meant my conversation with Clay was on hold until he was done. It said something about how messed up my mind was that I didn't even consider going into the bathroom to appreciate the view. I may not have been sleeping with him anymore, but I wasn't blind. The man was hot.

My brain chose that moment to flash a snapshot of last night in front of my eyes. A snapshot of the look in Jalen's eyes just before he'd kissed me. A shiver ran through me, and it wasn't because my hair was still wet.

I tightened the belt on my robe and pushed memories of sex aside. It was time for breakfast. I hadn't eaten much last night, especially after Clay's little announcement, and now I was hungry for something substantial.

Pancakes.

Pancakes with strawberries.

Yes.

I rummaged through my cabinets, pulling out various ingredients and setting them on the counter. Pancakes were one of the few things I knew how to make from scratch and focusing on small tasks helped me not think about anything else. I'd just finished filling two plates when I heard the shower turn off.

The best thing about not sleeping with Clay anymore was that I didn't feel the least bit guilty for leaving his pancakes on the counter and starting on mine. I'd only taken a few bites when someone knocked on the door.

Shit. I'd forgotten to call Adare and let her know how things were going. She had a spare key, but I knew she'd never use it unless it was an emergency. I left my plate and headed for the door. I didn't bother seeing who it was, and the moment I opened the door, I told myself that I really needed to start checking before I opened it.

"Rona." Jalen's face was flushed, the skin under his eyes smudged dark. "May I come in?"

I stared at him as I stepped to the side. What was he doing here? Yesterday, he hadn't been able to get away from me fast enough. I hadn't asked him to stay, and we weren't in a relationship. Sure, it'd been a shitty thing to do, but it hadn't really been much more than an anonymous hook-up. I barely knew him.

"It's early, Jalen," I said finally, crossing my arms. It hadn't felt weird, walking around in my robe with Clay here, but with Jalen, I felt...naked. "Couldn't this have waited until I was at the office?"

He shook his head. "This isn't about this case. I came to apologize. For leaving the way I did after...you know."

"I-It's—"

"Wow, something smells amazing."

I looked over to see Clay coming out of the bathroom with just a towel around his waist and a grin on his face. A couple months ago, seeing those broad shoulders and flat stomach would've turned me on, but now, I had a basic appreciation for his form, and that was all.

He nodded at Jalen. "Hey."

Jalen's features turned to ice. "Hey." He turned to me, his voice as cold as his expression. "I hadn't realized I was just the first in line last night."

"Excuse me?" I stared at him, hoping I'd misunderstood. "That's a hell of an apology."

He laughed, a sharp, bitter sound. "I wanted to apologize because I thought leaving without saying anything was rude. I should have known when you didn't call me, pissed off about my behavior, that you'd had other plans."

"What's going on, Rona?" Clay asked, looking back and forth between the two of us.

Jalen glanced at him, then turned back to me. "Did you shower before you fucked him, or does it turn him on, getting sloppy seconds?"

Mother. Fucker.

I grabbed the front of his shirt and yanked him toward the door. "I don't know if you think having money means you can talk to people like that, or that fucking me one time means you own me, but I don't care about whatever the hell your damage is. Stay the fuck away from me."

I shoved him out onto the landing, a part of me was hoping he hit a patch of ice and fell down the stairs. I slammed the door shut and stayed there for a moment, resting my forehead on the door as I worked to control my temper.

"Who the hell was that?" Clay's voice held a familiar, protective note. "And what was he talking about, being the 'first in line?'"

I straightened and took a slow breath. I needed to be careful how I handled this. The last thing I needed was for Clay to go after Jalen for being an ass. Clay was an FBI agent, and assaulting a civilian for insulting a friend wasn't something the agency would look on too highly.

"Don't worry about it," I said as I turned around. The smile on my face felt as plastic as it was, but it was better than any real expression would be. "It's done, and we have pancakes that are getting cold."

Clay looked like he wanted to press for more information, but he knew me well enough that it wouldn't do any good. "Let me get some clothes on."

As he picked up his shirt from the floor and headed back into the bathroom, I wondered if I should call Adare and tell her what happened. Then I imagined the look on her face if I told her how badly I'd fucked things up.

Better to leave well enough alone.

SEVENTEEN

Working on Meka's case kept my mind from wandering too much. This wasn't some simple case of investigating a possibly – *usually* – cheating spouse. This was a missing teenager. Too important for me to be distracted by some spoiled rich asshole who thought he could do and say whatever he wanted.

Fortunately, I'd always been good at compartmentalizing.

I put the last note into place on the whiteboard and then took a couple steps back, so I could see the big picture. I'd put all the information about Sylph Industries on the left and everything from the school on the right, then a picture of Meka right in the center. Theo's name was right above it. Now I just needed to connect the dots, see the patterns.

One of the first things was to look at discrepancies. There weren't any on Theo's side. Everyone essentially said the same things about him. Good guy and all that. Nothing strange I could see in his finances, unless he had a hidden account in the Cayman Islands. He didn't spend more than he made, not more than the average person did anyway.

It was Meka who seemed to have two different sides to her. Parents didn't always know their kids as well as they thought they did. While I was sure there were some who were the same at home as they were with their friends, it wasn't unusual for an investigation to turn up secrets that made parents cringe and cry.

On the other hand, teenagers weren't always the most reliable witnesses when it came to their peers. Biases, jealousies, the simple fact of immaturity, all of those things came into play when they talked about other teens. But, sometimes, they saw more than the adults in their lives.

Which meant I had to figure out the actual truth. Was Meka the girl that her father thought she was? Or was she a secret rebel? Sleeping around with different guys?

I looked at her picture, as if that would tell me what type of young woman she was. It wasn't a candid shot, but I'd seen plenty of those on her social media accounts. Those had shown her to be a fun-loving girl, but nothing that suggested the sort of behavior some of the boys in her class had attributed to her.

She didn't have a best friend. There wasn't one girl who claimed to be closer to her than anyone else. No one person in whom she'd confide.

Which meant, I suddenly realized, that she had to have put her feelings somewhere. If she didn't have a person to tell everything to, and she didn't put all sorts of personal shit on her social media sites, she had to have something else.

A diary. Journal. Whatever she wanted to call it. Maybe

she used pictures instead of words, but she had to have an outlet somewhere. I just needed to find it.

———

"I DON'T UNDERSTAND why Shawn keeps pushing for sex. I told him when he first asked me out that I wasn't ready. He said it was okay. That he'd wait because I was special. I told him that if he couldn't handle it, he should break up with me. I even tried breaking up with him, but he didn't want to hear it. He just kept saying that he was fine going at my pace, but then when we were alone, it was all 'come on, baby, I love you, don't you want to make me feel good.'"

I read the journal entry out loud to make sure I wasn't reading things into it.

Theo had let me into Meka's room but warned me that he'd looked for clues already. I'd thanked him and then found the diary ten minutes later. Not really a surprise since I'd found it under her bras and panties. Very few dads would be willing to go digging through his daughter's underwear drawer.

A cop probably would've found it, if any of them had bothered to take this case seriously, and maybe they'd even connect things the same way I had, but none of them could do what I was about to do. Shawn was a minor. They'd need to follow all sorts of legal procedures before they could even talk to him, and there was still a chance that he wouldn't know where Meka was.

I planned to cut out the middleman and go straight to the source. If he thought that I had to follow all those same rules, he was going to say things he never would have said otherwise. If those things led me to Meka, then it wouldn't matter how I'd gotten the information. She could tell the cops exactly what happened to her, and if it implicated Shawn, then he'd be toast.

And my gut told me that little slime-bag was at the center of the whole damn thing.

Which was why I was waiting outside the school on Friday afternoon, watching for that scruffy blond hair. I heard the bell ring, and I pushed myself off my car to stand straighter. A gust of wind made me pull my jacket closer, but I didn't even think about getting back into the car, not before I had a little chat with Shawn.

A couple students gave me funny looks but considering the condition of the side of my face, I didn't blame them. At some schools, seeing a woman with a bruised face wouldn't be cause for a second thought, but I had a feeling that wasn't the case here. This place was too nice to let all that out into the open. This was the sort of place where dirty secrets were kept in closets or under rugs where they belonged, never to be aired in public.

I didn't think too much more on that because I'd spotted him. That cocky little swagger and smirk didn't look any different from what I'd seen yesterday. Hopefully, that'd change in a moment.

I didn't call out to him or go running toward him. I didn't want to make a scene, not like that. I walked toward him, my pace nice and even, like I knew exactly where I was going but wasn't in too much of a rush to get there. I didn't stare at him but rather kept him in my line of sight as I pretended to casually look around. When I was a few feet away, I picked up speed, closing the distance rapidly as Shawn stopped to talk to a pretty blonde. She saw me first.

"Is she one of those bitches you said dug you?" Shawn turned when I spoke, and I grabbed his arm. "You can get back to riding her when I'm done with you. If she still wants you after I rip your balls off and cram them down your throat."

"Hey, hey, woman, what's your deal?!" He stumbled as I yanked him away from the blonde. "You can't manhandle me like this!"

I shoved him back against a tree and ignored the muttering behind me. People were watching, but I didn't care, not if it helped me get Meka back.

"I'm gonna have your badge, bitch!"

"Listen up, *bitch*," I snapped, "because I'm only saying this once. I'm not a cop. I'm not required to read you your rights or treat you like anything other than the piece of shit you are."

Fear flickered behind his eyes. "I can still call the cops on you."

"Yes, you can," I agreed. "And we'll have a nice little chat about the drugs in your backpack."

The color drained from his face. "The what?"

It'd been a guess based on his bloodshot eyes and general demeanor, but apparently a good one.

"I don't care about the shit you poison yourself with," I said. "I care about Meka and where she is. You tell me what you know, and maybe I won't make an anonymous call to your principal...and the local police department."

He glanced around, squirming nervously. "Not here, all right? I got a reputation."

"I'd think getting your ass handed to you by a woman would improve the way people think of you." I wanted to stay here and make him look like an even bigger asshole, but I didn't know what he was going to tell me. If it was something that would embarrass Meka, I didn't want the whole school finding out. I sighed. "My car's over here."

I didn't let go of his arm, practically dragging him to my car. I had a feeling he was going to spread around some seedy lie about how I blew him or some shit like that, but I didn't care. If a couple rumors floating around a high school were the price I had to pay for finding Meka, it'd be worth it.

I shoved the kid into the back seat and climbed in after him. "Talk."

He crossed his arms, looking even more like a sulking child than he already had. "Look, I got a rep to keep up, and she was hurting it. Being a damn prick tease. I took her out three times." He held up three fingers. "Everyone knows that a girl got to give it up on the third date, but she just kept saying she wasn't ready, or some shit like that. I told her fine, I'd be good if she went down. She was lucky. No dude's gonna shell out cash for three dates if he ain't getting some that third time."

I couldn't resist. I smacked the back of his head. "Real classy."

He shrugged even as he glared at me. "Anyway, she wouldn't do nothing. Not even a handy."

"Shawn," I warned.

His cool-guy demeanor shifted, and he looked uneasy for the first time since I'd met him. "Look, these dudes are seri-ous. I was getting my...medicine when I made a joke and then they held me to it. These ain't the sort of dudes you wanna mess with. Believe me."

"What joke?"

His eyes shifted, and he looked paler than only moments ago. "Just let it go. When these girls is gone, they gone."

"I'm losing my patience, and that doesn't bode well for you, Shawn." I took my phone out of my pocket. "Maybe I should call my friend at the FBI."

His entire face morphed into panic. "You don't have no–"

"I do," I said while tapping buttons. "Keep giving me the runaround and you'll meet him up close and personal."

"All right, all right." He held up his hands. "I'll tell you everything. You said you ain't a cop, right?"

"I'm not."

"My supplier got locked up almost a year ago, so I started looking for another one. I found this guy who had primo stuff. Except after a couple weeks, he didn't want money. He wanted something I could get him. Girls."

My free hand clenched into a fist. Girls. Plural. I realized that he'd said that before too. I just hadn't caught it until now.

"Him and his guys wanted girls that no one would miss. They didn't need to be pretty or skinny or anything. Just high schoolers. And losers. Not so many that people would notice, but whenever they said they wanted one, I had to do it."

"Hate to tell you, but a whole lot of people noticed Meka was missing."

"Yeah, I fucked that up." He scratched the back of his head. "That last night, I made everything perfect. Dinner. Flowers. I shelled out serious cash. And she still said no. Bitch needed to learn a lesson, and they needed a girl."

M. S. PARKER

"You gave your girlfriend to human traffickers because she wouldn't have sex with you?"

He scowled. "It sounds all kinds of shady when you say it like that."

"It's pathological, you moron," I snapped. A couple pieces clicked into place. "Did you tell them that I was looking for her?"

He shrugged yet again, but the guilt was plastered on his face. Now I knew why I'd been attacked, and how they'd known where I was. He was lucky I was more concerned with Meka than my own safety.

"Where is she, asshole?"

"I don't know." He shrugged. "Seriously. I take the girl to meet the guys. I get my stash. They get the girl."

I reminded myself that it wouldn't be a good idea to knock Shawn out. Delivering him to the cops would have to be justice enough.

"Where do you meet them? The same place every time, or do you go somewhere different?"

"It's one of those storage places," he said. "On the edge of the city."

I pulled my notebook out of my pocket. "Address. Now."

He hesitated, then rattled it off. "Just don't tell them you got it from me, okay? You might not be a cop, but they don't like people sticking their noses in their business, you know?"

Oh, I knew. And I had no doubt that they were going to be royally pissed when they figured out I wasn't just coming for Meka. I'd get her, but then I was going to burn the whole damn thing to the ground.

But first, this asshole was going to jail.

EIGHTEEN

THIS WAS A BAD IDEA. I KNEW IT WAS A BAD IDEA. HELL, a six-year-old would've known this was a bad idea. I was by myself, still healing, and didn't really know what I was about to find.

But I'd be damned if I let Meka be missing for a single second longer if I could find her now.

Which was why I parked my car at one of the first storage units, then walked down to the unit number Shawn had given me. The guy in the booth at the front had barely looked up when I pulled in, so I doubted he'd even notice that I hadn't gone inside that first unit, or that I'd started down toward the other end.

Once I was out of sight, I kept to the shadows, my heart pounding harder with every step I took. The adrenaline coursing through my system was in part due to the highly stupid thing I was doing, but another part was the anticipation of doing something important. Finally. The sort of work I'd always thought I'd do with the FBI.

I'd done a couple cases with Adare, but none of them had been the sort of cases that made a difference like this one. Cheating spouses. Missing pets. Deadbeat parents who owed child support. Those were the bread and butter of private investigators. Something like this, where it wasn't just about finding a single missing girl. If what Shawn had told me was true, this could make a huge difference in so many lives.

I was only a few yards away when I saw the black van parked around the far side of the building. Probably not empty then. I'd taken a couple hours to do some research on the place, and I knew there were a total of three entrances. The giant double doors where people could take things in and out. The main door to the office. And an emergency exit in the back.

It was that door I went to now.

A few months before my uncle died, I'd come home from college for a long weekend and found the two of them, half-drunk, trying to pick every lock they could find. I hadn't joined in the drinking – between being underage and Clay being an FBI agent, alcohol seemed like a bad idea – but I had listened and learned. The three of us had brought it up again when they were sober, and the lessons had gone on a couple more times.

Which meant when I came to the emergency exit, it didn't take me long to see it was locked from the outside but unlocked on the inside. I took my lock-picking kit out of my pocket and got to work. I was technically breaking and entering, and if I'd been a cop or FBI agent, that would've been an issue. Now, I could go to jail if someone reported me, but I was sure I was going to find one of two things: nothing at all, or people doing things a hell of a lot more illegal than I was.

I let out a breath as the pins clicked into place and then slowly eased the door open. I paused, listening before I went inside. For a few seconds, I couldn't hear anything, and then I heard a soft sound. Soft sounds. More than one. Girls were crying.

Shit.

I went inside, moving slowly despite the urgency building inside me. I didn't know what was waiting for me up ahead, and I couldn't let my emotions rule my behavior. I might not have to worry about preserving chains of evidence and getting search warrants, but if anyone got hurt because of my impatience, I'd never forgive myself.

When I reached the end of the short corridor, I was at the corner where a small office and single stall bathroom sat to the left, the main area to the right. The room was full of large, unopened boxes, giving me cover as I moved toward the sounds.

Then I saw them.

Five girls of high school age were huddled together, sniffling and crying. From where I was hiding, I couldn't see all of their faces, but I could see the profile of the girl who was above the others. The girl who had placed herself on the outside of the group and kept looking over toward where my peripheral vision had registered a handful of armed men.

I'd get to them in a moment.

I needed a moment to let it sink in. I'd found Meka. She was alive, and it appeared, unharmed. She was dirty and looked like she'd been crying during the time she'd been here, but her clothes were on and not ripped.

I hoped that meant good things.

Then it was time to figure out how to handle things from

here because I counted at least four men with weapons. I'd never be able to get all of the girls out of here safely. Not by myself.

Shit. *Shit.*

I looked down at my phone and tried to power it on, but the screen remained as black as my hope. The battery was dead. I couldn't call for help, so I needed to go back to the police station.

Dammit!

"WHAT DO you mean you let him go?"

The desk sergeant sighed. "Look, all I know is that his dad showed up with a lawyer, and ten minutes later, they were all leaving together."

"He's been giving girls to sex traffickers in exchange for drugs, and he just walked out?" I was getting louder, but I didn't care. Shawn had told me exactly what he'd done, and I'd given his statement to the cops, along with an audio file of the recording I had of the conversation.

"Miss, I'm not one of the officers on the case. All I know is what I told you."

"Who were the officers on the case?" I asked.

"Who'd you speak with before?"

I pinched the bridge of my nose and reminded myself that he was just doing his job. "Officer Lennard."

"Lennard's still here." He jerked his thumb over his shoulder. When he saw the surprised look on my face, he added, "Guy's a pain in my ass. Someone needs to bug him for a change."

"Glad to help," I said as I walked past the sergeant.

After a few feet, I was able to recognize the stout, middle-aged man I'd talked to before. Before, I'd assumed that the vibe I'd gotten off him was his disgust at what Shawn had done, but now I wondered if he had an issue with work, or with me.

"Officer Lennard?"

He raised his head, scowling as he saw me. "That kid's family is going to sue your ass off and don't think for a minute I'm going to defend you."

"I don't care about him right now," I said. I didn't add that I'd make sure someone heard about it later, but for the moment, Shawn wasn't foremost on my mind. "I found Meka Ludwick."

"Who?"

"The fifteen-year-old who's been missing for a week," I said, grinding my teeth together. "The one *that kid* gave to sex traffickers because she wouldn't sleep with him."

"There's no evidence he did anything," Lennard said, "and some half-assed, forced confession doesn't cut it. Tomorrow, I'll probably be arresting *you* on attempted kidnapping and other charges."

I made a dismissive gesture. "You've got to be kidding me." I blew out a harsh breath. "Listen, I found Meka and at least four other girls being held prisoner by several armed men. We need to go rescue them now before they're moved."

"And how did you come about this information?" He leaned back in his chair, as if he needed to make it more obvious that the concept of actual police work was foreign to him.

"It doesn't matter," I snapped. "This isn't about search

warrants or anything like that. These girls are in serious danger, and I'm reporting it to you in the hopes that you'll get off your ass and get them."

He leaned forward then, round face flushing. "Listen here, you can't come in here making all sorts of wild accusations and insulting officers of the law. I know who you are, Rona Quick."

"That's good," I fired back, "because I know who you are too. You're the one I'm going to tell Theo Ludwick to sue if anything else happens to his daughter. For all you know, Shawn could've called his buddies as soon as he left here, and they're in the process of moving the girls somewhere more secure."

He shook his head, a smug smirk curling his lips. "No, you don't get it. I know who you are. You see, I have a buddy in Denver who called down here a couple hours ago to tell me I had some wanna-be FBI agent going rogue on my turf."

"I'm a private investigator," I said, keeping my face carefully blank. "I have a license, and I was legally hired to find Meka Ludwick because someone here didn't want to do their job. If you would've done the work in the first place, I wouldn't have been involved."

"If you think I'm going to let someone the Feds kicked out of training tell me how to do my job, you got another thing coming." He pointed at me, then slammed his hand on his desk. "Girls like that get themselves into trouble. We have more important cases to work than some girl who slept with half the school."

"'Girls like that,'" I repeated. "I thought you didn't know who Meka was, or the rumors about her."

His face was starting to turn a disturbing shade of red,

and I wondered if I'd be legally obligated to do CPR if he had a heart attack.

I cursed my phone and its dead battery, then cursed myself for not thinking to charge it. None of this would be happening if I'd been able to just call 911. I said as much to the asshole in front of me.

"You do that, and I'll arrest you for obstruction, filing a false police report, and anything else I can get to stick." He pointed toward the door. "Get your ass out of here before I decide to arrest you right now."

I looked around the room, but the handful of other police who were here all had their eyes on their desks like whatever they were working on was more important than whether or not I had vital information. I knew that not all of the police in the city were like Lennard or the ones who wouldn't even look at me, but these were definitely leaving a bad taste in my mouth.

But now wasn't the time to deal with them. I had to find someone who would listen to me. Someone who'd help get Meka out, no matter what. And as much as I hated it, there was only one person I could think of who'd forgive me for knocking on his door at five in the morning and who had the sort of power that I'd need to rescue the girls. At least someone who wasn't two hours away. I needed help now, and I didn't know how long it'd take Clay to round up the cavalry.

Shit.

I really did have only one choice.

And I *really* didn't want to talk to him, but the alternative wasn't an option I could live with.

Dammit.

NINETEEN

I took a deep breath as I ran up the steps to the front door of a beautiful, sprawling house. Only a few streets over from where Jenna and Rylan lived, I now realized I hadn't fully appreciated how rich Jalen was until this very moment. It was one thing to know that he'd sold his first company for a large, undisclosed sum. It was something else entirely to see what he'd been able to do with the money.

Fortunately, that just made me feel even better about what I was doing now. He had the sort of money and public face needed to get things done. Since he was the one who hired me, I didn't feel guilty about talking to him before telling Theo I'd found Meka. Besides, if something went wrong, it would crush Theo if I gave him hope that the worst was almost over.

I knocked on the door and waited. I twisted my fingers together as I mentally ran through what I wanted to say. Because of how things had gone the last time we'd been together, I knew he'd most likely tell me to get lost, which meant I needed to get him to understand that I wasn't here for me before he slammed the door in my face. Those girls couldn't afford for more time to be wasted.

I had my mouth open, ready to give Jalen a rapid-fire list of all the reasons he needed to help me, but when the door opened...it wasn't Jalen.

She was tall, but not quite as tall as me, slender, almost too much though, but none of that was my business. It didn't matter that I now recognized her as a model I'd seen on bill-boards and magazines all over the country. Elise Marx, if I remembered correctly. Long, chestnut brown hair, the sort of dark eyes that men wrote about. She was gorgeous.

"Who are you?" She crossed her arms as if my being here was interrupting something important. Her beauty sleep, no doubt. Although from the looks of her, she didn't need much of that.

I ignored the fact that, for all Jalen's talk when he'd seen Clay, it hadn't taken *him* long to fill his bed. That wasn't why I was here though. He was an ass, and I didn't want that drama in my life. I wasn't here for me, or even for Jalen, really. I was here for Meka and the other girls. Jalen was a means to an end.

"My name's Rona Quick. Jalen hired me to find...hired me to do some research for him. Is he here?"

She gave me a tight smile. "My husband isn't available right now."

Husband?

Okay, now I was pissed. That asshole had made me part of an affair. But again, not the point of me being there. I could be furious with him later, when this was all done.

"I need to talk to him."

"What you *need* is to walk your ass out of here and never even look at my husband again." She gave me one of those up and down looks that women like her always used on women like me. "I don't care what promises he made you or how special you think your connection was. He's mine, and nothing's going to change that."

I took a slow, deliberate breath, and then let it out. "I need to speak to Jalen about his case. It's urgent."

"Elise."

Jalen's voice came from behind her and color flooded her cheeks. "I'm taking care of it, Jalen."

"I need to talk to you about Meka." I raised my voice so that he'd be able to hear me.

"Who's Meka?" Elise snapped. "Some other woman you've been fucking? The three of you, all together? Is that what you've been doing?"

"Meka's none of your fucking business, Elise." Jalen appeared at her side. "Don't you have somewhere else to be?"

Damn. I didn't like the woman but seeing how coldly he was treating her actually made me have some sympathy. At least I knew it wasn't just me he behaved like that with.

After he helped me get the cops involved, I planned on never seeing him again. He'd get my invoice in the mail, with a request to drop the check in the mail rather than bring it to the office.

"Jalen." Elise's voice had taken on a whiny quality that she was far too old to be using. She was probably only a few years older than me, but I was about twenty years too old to talk like that.

"Now, Elise."

"I need my purse before I can go." She stormed back into the house.

"You said you're here about Meka?" Jalen looked in my general direction, but not directly at me.

If I'd cared, I would've thought that he looked embarrassed.

But I didn't care, so there was that. I didn't care that he was wearing a pair of flannel pants and a t-shirt that made him look far too good for this early in the morning. Or that just the sight of him made me remember what it had been like to have him inside me.

"I am, but if you're busy—"

"Come inside. It's cold out there."

I stared at him. What the fuck? He was acting like the other night hadn't happened.

Then Elise shoved past us both, and I reminded myself to keep my focus where it belonged. On Meka.

"Don't mind her," Jalen said as he walked back into the house. "I'm glad you're here. We need to talk."

I followed. "I told your wife—"

"About that—"

"I don't care," I cut him off again. "I really am here about Meka. I need your help."

"What happened?" His entire demeanor changed, and I knew he had his focus in the right place now.

"To get right to the point, Meka's asshole boyfriend sold her for drugs. He gave me the address where he took her. I went there—"

"Alone?" His head snapped around. "That wasn't smart, Rona."

I held up a hand. "Not your business and not the time. I

found Meka and at least five other girls. They were being held in a storage unit by several armed guys. Contrary to what you might think, I'm not stupid. I knew I couldn't get all of the girls out safely, so I went to the cops, but they aren't going to do anything."

"What do you mean they aren't going to do anything?"

I leaned against the back of an overstuffed chair. I was exhausted, but I still had, as they say, 'miles to go before I sleep.'

"I took the boyfriend down to the station after he confessed what he did, but they let him go. My phone was dead, so I couldn't call for help, and when I went to the station to tell them what I found, Officer Lennard basically blew me off, acting like I was trying to interfere in a police investigation. He actually threatened to arrest me."

"I've never liked that slimy bastard," Jalen muttered. He looked at me, a hard glint in his eyes. "You need me to pull some strings to get the cops to that storage place?"

"I'm afraid they're going to take the girls somewhere else," I said, worry worming down my spine. Too much time had already passed, and I'd never forgive myself if I lost track of the girls because I hadn't charged my stupid phone. "Shawn could have already warned them. He's the one who tipped them off that I was looking in the first place. I thought about going back myself, but it's not something one person can pull off, not without risking everyone's lives."

Jalen already had his phone up to his ear. I would've been annoyed that he seemed to be ignoring me, but he was doing exactly what I needed.

"Hey, Chet, it's Jalen."

It took me a moment to realize that he was talking to the

Police Commissioner, Chet Shumaker III.

"I need to call in a favor. There's something going on at King's Storage, unit twelve. I can't tell you how I know, but I can tell you that if you send some men out there, prepared to take down some pretty nasty guys, and have a couple ambulances waiting, you'll end up being a hero. Great press to use when you start your campaign for governor in a couple years."

Smart, using the commissioner's political ambitions to get him to do the right thing. I could see the business side of Jalen in that small conversation.

"Yes, this needs to be done now. I know it's early, but it's time sensitive." He waited a few seconds, then smiled. "Excellent. Thank you, Chet. And yes, if you could give me a call when it's taken care of, I'd appreciate it." He set the phone down and looked at me. "It's done."

"Thank you." The words were said on the exhale of a relieved breath. "I'll head down to the site, and once I see Meka, I'll give Theo a call. I'll send you a bill after that."

"Wait," he said before I was even able to turn to go. "You can't go there. It could compromise the rescue."

Dammit. I didn't think I would, but as soon as he put the idea out there, it was all I could think about. "Good point. I'll go to the police station then."

"Wait here with me," Jalen said. "You can find out what happened when Chet calls me. And we can talk."

I bristled at that. "We don't have anything to talk about."

His expression was serious as he walked over to me. "Yes, we do."

I swallowed hard and nodded. Apparently, we were going to talk.

TWENTY

THE ADRENALINE THAT HAD KEPT ME GOING FOR MORE than a day was starting to wear off, but I'd gone for longer periods of time on less sleep. I'd make it this time too.

Especially since I was now sitting next to Jalen on a very comfortable couch, preparing to talk about whatever he thought we needed to talk about.

"I'm sorry."

Okay, after the way he'd talked to me and to his wife, I hadn't expected an apology to be the first thing out of his mouth when he sat down.

He handed me a cup of coffee. "I already had the coffee going, so you might as well take advantage of it."

I took a drink and sighed as the heat and caffeine flowed through me. "Thank you."

"For the coffee or the apology?"

"The coffee. I'm still not sure about the apology," I answered honestly.

He took another long drink of his own coffee and then set

the mug down on the table in front of us. "I was wrong. A lot. I was wrong to kiss you, to have sex with you, to leave you like that."

"Wait." I held up a hand. "You don't get to unilaterally decide that us kissing and having sex was wrong by itself. It took two of us, and I was all in for that decision. How you handled the after part, yeah, I'll take your apology for that." And I wasn't even about to bring up the wife part. Yet.

"You were hurt," he began. "I should have–"

"I'm an adult, and I knew what I was doing." I shrugged. "Besides, it's not like you were the only hook up I'd ever had."

His mouth flattened into a line, and something hot flashed across his eyes. "I figured that out already."

I raised an eyebrow. "Really? The married man is going to bring up *my* personal life?"

"I'm not married," he said, his mouth twisting into a scowl. "Not anymore."

"So, Elise Marx is–?"

"My ex-wife." He glanced toward the front door. "Or at least she will be as soon as she signs the damn papers."

"I hate to say it, Jalen, but until a divorce is finalized, you're still married."

He made a frustrated sound. "Look, I was twenty-one when we met. We dated for four crazy years, and then I decided it was a good idea for us to get married. It was good for ten months, and then she walked out. We separated for six months, then tried to reconcile." His voice was flat, like he was reciting a series of historical events rather than telling me about a romantic relationship in his past. "We were working on it for a few months when I found her in bed with one of the bodyguards I'd hired to keep her safe."

Ouch.

"She won't sign the divorce papers because she's insisting that the adultery clause in the prenuptial agreement hasn't applied since she walked out ten months into the marriage." His hand scraped against the stubble on his jaw. "She's being a pain in my ass, but I was wrong to take my issues with her out on you."

"That's why you freaked out when you saw Clay," I said softly. "It brought up a lot of bad memories."

"Like I said, I was wrong. I had no right to take all of that out on you." His hand went through his hair, leaving clumps standing up all over his head. "Hell, I don't even have the right to be jealous at all. We weren't – *aren't* – in a relationship. What you do and who you do it with isn't my business, and my behavior was inexcusable. I'm sorry."

I gave him a partial smile. "If I'm honest, Jalen, I have to say that I had a flash of that inappropriate jealousy when Elise introduced herself as your wife."

He shot me a sideways look. "Really?"

I glared at him. "Let's not get distracted here."

He laughed, and the energy around us shifted from angry and tense to something warmer. "You caught me off-guard from moment one, Rona Quick. You weren't anything I was expecting, and that day, seeing you hurt, it brought things to the surface that I wasn't ready for."

Something in my stomach fluttered as I admitted, "I didn't expect you either. And nothing happened with Clay and me. In the past, yes, he and I were involved, but not anymore. We'd been friends, had a casual thing, and then we're back to being friends. He came to talk to me, and I didn't want him driving back to Denver so late. That's all."

"Elise showed up here at midnight, drunk and ranting. I let her stay in one of the guest rooms to sleep it off." He sighed. "I haven't been in love with her for a long time, if I ever really had, but that doesn't mean I want her to hurt herself."

I reached for my coffee and finished with a single long gulp. It wasn't quite cold, but definitely heading toward lukewarm. I needed the caffeine though.

Actually, I needed something stronger than caffeine. I needed alcohol. Clearing things up with Jalen had been good, but now I was all too aware that we were waiting for a phone call that was either going to close my case or make things a whole lot worse.

And I didn't know what to do.

Should I just sit here and stare at the phone? Would it be wrong to want to take a nap? Then I remembered that I was at Jalen's house and taking a nap here would be weird. No nap then. Should we talk? About what? The case? I'd given him pretty much everything I had already. And talking about it would make me start to think about what those poor girls were going through, which would make me want to go down to the storage unit and help. Except I couldn't help. Because I wasn't a cop or an FBI agent.

Because I'd gotten kicked out for lying about my name and about my shitty dad spending life in prison.

Which meant I couldn't go in and help the girls I found or arrest the scumbags who'd been hurting them. I hadn't even been able to get the people whose job it was to protect them to go and do just that.

I swallowed hard, tears burning my eyes. No. I wasn't going to do this now. I couldn't do this now. Not with Jalen sitting there. We'd just gotten things fixed up between us. I didn't need to make things awkward because I was too tired to control my emotions.

"Can we move past what happened?" Jalen broke the silence. "Go back before I acted like a total ass and start over again?"

I cleared my throat and pushed down the emotions threatening to choke me. "So, before we met then?"

He chuckled. "How about before I walked out like a moron?"

I raised an eyebrow, grateful for the distraction. "You mean back to when we were fucking?"

He leaned closer, his arm brushing against mine. "Yes, Rona. Back to when I was buried balls deep in that tight cunt of yours, coming so hard I saw stars."

F-u-c-k.

"Yes," I whispered. "I think we can go back to that."

I really hoped he meant what I thought he did. It was stupid. Again. But I wanted it. I *needed* it. Him. Not just for a distraction, but because there was something I didn't understand between us, and I wasn't strong enough to stay away.

"I don't want to take advantage of the situation," he said quietly. He brushed hair back from my face but didn't pull his hand back. His fingers ghosted across my skin, a touch nearly impossible to feel, but one that left such a fire in its wake that I couldn't feel anything else.

"I don't want pity sex," I countered. I put my hand on his thigh, loving the feel of his muscles bunching beneath my palm.

"I don't pity you, Rona." He slid his hand up and around

to grip my hair. The shock of pain prompted a small sound that made his pupils dilate, his irises darken. "I admire you."

"You *admire* me?"

He shook his head and chuckled, a sensual sound that flowed over my skin. "Yes, crazy woman. I admire you. Everything you've accomplished. How strong you are."

"That's what all the girls want to hear." I tucked my hands under his shirt, my smile widening as he cursed. "How strong they are."

He leaned closer, not stopping until his mouth was only a breath away from mine. "I thought women wanted the truth." He brushed his lips across mine. "That's the truth. You're strong."

He kissed the corner of my mouth.

"And insanely intelligent. Passionate. Stubborn. Sexy."

He pulled my head to the side and kissed down the side of my neck.

"I don't pity you," he repeated his earlier statement as he raised his head. His gaze burned into me. "I *want* you because you're all of those things I said and more. I'm not asking for anything more than this right now if that's what you want. All I need to know now is if you want me too."

I answered him by sliding off the couch and down onto my knees. "Shirt off."

He had it off in one smooth motion, revealing all of that gorgeous flesh. As I positioned myself between his legs, I ran my hands up his stomach, admiring the tight muscles and light dusting of hair. I scratched my nails across his flat nipples, and he swore, his body jerking.

"Shit, Rona," he groaned. "Your turn. Take off your shirt."

I ignored him, turning my attention to the growing bulge

that his soft cotton pants did absolutely nothing to hide. He raised his hips, helping me get rid of the last barrier between me and my prize.

And what a prize.

The man was a work of art, and I took the time to drink in the sight of him, naked and all mine. His cock lay heavy on his thigh, thickening, but not yet fully aroused. It was time to help him with that.

I wrapped my hand around the base of his shaft, lightly stroking him from root to tip. I'd touched other men before, but it never failed to amaze me at just how soft the skin was on such a delicate part of the body. No, I decided. *Delicate* was the wrong word. There was nothing *delicate* about what I held in my hand.

I ran my nail along the underside of his cock, tracing the vein that ran there, pumping blood into his growing erection. *Sensitive* was a better word.

He muttered something under his breath, and I looked up at him. "What was that?"

"I said you are killing me." He smiled. "But I don't mind."

"I'm just getting started," I warned him.

I held him in one hand as I licked his skin, the bitter tang of salt and musk exploding on my tongue. I'd never really minded oral sex, but I didn't think I'd ever enjoyed it as much as I was enjoying it now. It was more than the physical sensation of taking him into my mouth, more than the feel of the tip slipping past my lips and over my tongue. It was the sounds he made, those throaty groans and primal grunts, each one turning me on even more.

I cupped his balls, rolling them between my fingers as I moved my mouth and hand in tandem. I swirled my tongue around the tip of his cock, then sucked on it like it was some sort of treat. Maybe it was. I enjoyed myself during sex, but this was different. He wanted to take charge. I could feel it. The fact that he was holding back intrigued me, and that wasn't something I experienced too often.

He cursed, running his hand through my hair, strong fingers massaging my scalp before pushing down just hard enough for me to know what he wanted. I went lower, taking him deeper. My mouth stretched painfully wide, jaw aching, but I let his cock slide to the back of my throat, holding as much of him in my mouth as I could.

"Fuck, Rona!"

He yanked me up by my hair, the pain sending tears to my eyes even as I coughed and gasped. Before I could catch my breath, he hauled me up on his lap, his arms tight around me.

"I'm sorry," he said hoarsely. "I shouldn't have–"

I grabbed the back of his head and slammed my mouth onto his, cutting off the rest of the sentence. His cock was hot and hard against my leg, and his hands moved down to palm my ass, grinding me against him. At least I knew he still wanted me. Judging by the way his hips were jerking against me, he *really* wanted me.

I bit down on his lip, and he growled, the sound going straight through me.

"Careful. You might not like what happens if you keep that up."

I reached down between us and wrapped my fingers around his cock. "Maybe I'll like it a lot."

His eyes narrowed as he looked up at me, and then he flipped us over. His hands went to my pants, yanking them and my underwear off in one quick motion. He tossed them over his shoulder and reached for my shirt.

"No."

He stopped and gave me a curious look.

"If that changes things–"

He leaned over me, the hair on his legs rough against the insides of my thighs. "Do you still want this?"

I nodded without hesitation. My body was throbbing, and if I didn't get some relief from him, I'd have to take care of it myself, but he would do a hell of a lot better job.

In one smooth move, he grabbed my legs and slid down between my thighs. The moment his tongue touched me, a shudder ran through me and my eyes closed. Waves of blissful pleasure washed over me, each one stronger than the last. I'd known he had a skilled tongue, but this was above and beyond anything I could have imagined.

A spike of pain jolted me upright, and I glared down at Jalen. He grinned up at me, his expression as heated as my flushed skin. "I told you that you might not like what came next."

"Do it again."

His eyebrows went up in surprise. "Are you sure?"

I nodded, watching as he turned his head and sank his teeth into the flesh of my inner thigh. The shock of pain was expected this time, but it didn't make the intensity any less. And it definitely didn't make me enjoy it any less.

I'd always known that I liked things a little rough, but I'd never been able to ask anyone to go as far as I wanted. Jalen, it appeared, would do it without any qualms.

"Damn," he said as he slid a finger inside me. "You're soaked."

"Don't you have something better to do with that tongue?" I dropped my hand down between my legs. "Or do I have to do everything myself?"

He grabbed my hand. "You don't touch yourself unless I tell you to."

Shit, that was hot.

Then his mouth was on me again, his hands holding my hips tightly as his tongue worked its way inside me. He licked every inch of me, finding places no one had reached before, each one sending me higher, closer to the edge. When he slid two fingers inside me, his tongue dancing back and forth across my clit, I started to come.

And I kept coming as he crooked his fingers, rubbing against my g-spot until I was pushing at his hands, needing a different sort of relief.

He looked entirely too pleased with himself as he pushed up onto his knees but considering the fact that I still had mini-orgasms going off inside me, he wasn't exactly being immodest.

"Have you ever recorded yourself?" he asked as he ran his hands up my legs. "You should really see your face when you come. Gorgeous." He smirked. "Unless you only come like that for me."

"Come like what?" I tried for casual and failed spectacularly.

He leaned over me until his mouth was only inches from mine. "Like a fucking freight train."

I flushed, but the heat in his eyes told me he meant it as a compliment. "Maybe we should test the theory. See if you're as good with your cock as you are with your fingers and tongue."

"Challenge accepted." He took my mouth in a bruising kiss, his tongue thrusting into my mouth at the same time his cock entered me.

I dug my nails into his shoulders as I wrapped my legs around him. My heels thumped against his ass, urging him to move harder and faster. As if his strokes weren't already making me see stars. I scratched long stripes down his back, his body bucking against mine with each one.

"J," I panted, tearing my mouth from his. "I need I need I need I need..."

"Fucking tight," he grunted, his expression strained. "I'm going to..."

White spots danced in front of my eyes, and I tightened every muscle in my body.

"Fuck, Rona, fuck..." The last word turned into a groan, and a shudder ran through him. "I need you to go first. Please. I can't...please..."

It was the desperation in his voice that pushed me over the edge. I'd never had anyone need me like that. Not even Clay.

I didn't recognize the sound that came out of my mouth as I exploded. Scream. Cry. Wail. I should have been embarrassed, self-conscious, but I couldn't think about anything other than the pleasure coursing through me. I barely even registered Jalen's body stiffening above mine as he came, emptying inside me with pulse after pulse of cum.

There was something about that last bit that I needed to consider, but I would come back to it once my brain was functioning again. For right now, I gave myself over to the freight train rumbling over me.

TWENTY-ONE

"Shit, Rona, I'm sorry." Jalen had started apologizing about thirty seconds ago when he realized that he hadn't used a condom. I was trying to get a word in, but he kept looking down at me like he'd fucked up worse than before.

Finally, I put my hand over his mouth, stopping the next outpouring of words. "First, I appreciate the apology, but it's on both of us. We both got caught up in the moment. Second, I'm on the pill, and I'm clean, so no worries from my end."

"I am too," he said quickly. "I've gotten tested regularly after everything that went down with Elise."

I reached up and brushed his hair away from his face. He wasn't a business suit and insanely expensive haircut kind of guy, but he dressed nicely. Still, I had to admit, I preferred this rumpled, freshly fucked version of him.

"Then we write it off as impulsivity," I said matter-of-factly. "But no freak outs."

"Agreed." He stretched out next to me, hooking his arm around me to pull me back against his body.

I was a little surprised we fit. The couch wasn't huge, but it was bigger than average, probably because Jalen was bigger than average.

An understatement to say the least.

"Can I ask you a question?" He ran his hand over my hip and then down to the bare skin between my belly button and the aching place between my legs.

"You just came inside me," I teased. "I think I can handle a question."

"Both times we were together, you made it clear that you didn't want your shirt off."

I tensed but managed to keep my voice light. "That doesn't sound like a question."

"Is it like that with everyone...or just me?"

The trace of vulnerability in his voice was the only thing that kept me from telling him that it was none of his damn business. "Everyone."

After a second of silence, he nodded. "All right."

And that was it. I doubted his curiosity would be satisfied with my answer for long, but that was okay. This wasn't a relationship. It was comfort and distraction. That was all.

As if on cue, Jalen's phone rang.

He leaned over me to pick it up from next to his still half-full mug of coffee before sitting up to answer it. "Chet?"

I sat up and waited, watching his expression as he listened to what the commissioner had to say. The moment I saw relief on his features, a weight lifted off my shoulders. It was good news. I'd wait until I actually heard it to be completely at ease, but I felt far more hopeful than I had a moment before.

"Thanks, Chet. Yes, please pass along my thanks to the police department, and I'll see everyone at the annual ball later this year." As he ended the call, he turned toward me, a smile spreading across his face. "They got all of the girls out safely, all of the guys arrested without a shot fired. They confirmed Meka was there and gave her a phone to call her dad. They're all on their way to the hospital to be checked over, and Theo's going to meet them there."

I put my hands over my face as a surge of emotion threatened to overwhelm me. Meka was okay. The other girls were okay. They'd need to talk about what happened to them, get into counseling, but if we'd gotten to them in time to prevent any assaults, they'd be able to move past it. Have normal lives.

"You did great work," Jalen said softly as he put his hand on my shoulder. "You saved Meka, and you saved those girls."

I nodded but didn't trust myself to speak just yet. Since I'd gotten kicked out of training, I hadn't wanted to think much about how much I'd always wanted to help people, to save them. I'd known that I'd lost my chance when I'd lost the FBI, but now, I'd actually helped someone. *Real* help.

I needed a few minutes to compose myself. As I shifted, I became all too aware of what I wasn't wearing, as well as the mess between my legs. I needed to clean up.

"Up the stairs, second door on the left. Towels are in the linen closet next to the sink. Use whatever you need. Take as long as you need."

"Thanks," I whispered.

I couldn't look at him as I got up. We'd had amazing sex, and he didn't act weird this time. He didn't push when I didn't tell him the reason why I kept my shirt on. That, on top of the huge win with Meka, should've had me on cloud nine. Instead, I felt uneasy, like I'd gone a step too far, let him too close. We hadn't spent a lot of time together. Had sex twice. He wasn't my friend like Clay.

So why did I feel like he saw far more than I wanted him to?

It wasn't until I stepped under the showerhead that the white noise of water against skin drowned out the chaos in my head. I let the hot water soothe my aching muscles, drive away all of the confusion. It'd come back, I knew, but for right now, I was thankful for the quiet.

If I'd been at home, I probably would've taken a bath and fallen asleep, but that wasn't exactly the safest thing to do when I was this tired, which meant it was probably a good thing that I'd cleaned up here. It almost made up for the fact that his shampoo and soap had that faint spicy scent that immediately sent my mind back to the two of us on the couch. The feel of him. The smell.

I winced as I stepped out of the shower and mentally cursed myself for how rough things had gotten. Not because I hadn't wanted it, but because I was going to be feeling it for a while.

I was still drying myself off when I realized that I'd left my pants and underwear downstairs by the couch. Shit. Sure, I'd walked into the bathroom wearing only my bra and shirt, but it just felt weird to put those back on and return to the living room bare-assed. I should've thought things through better, but I'd been so overcome with so many emotions, I hadn't been thinking.

I set aside the towel and picked up my bra. I'd put it and

my shirt back on, then wrap the towel around my waist until I gathered my other clothes. Simple. As I began to put on my bra, I averted my eyes from my reflection like I always did.

I didn't need the reminders, especially right now.

"Rona, I thought you might want some clean clothes to wear home..." Jalen's voice trailed off as he opened the door... and saw what I'd hidden from everyone since I was thirteen years old.

The ugly, jagged scar that began right under my collarbone and went down between my breasts, then under the right side of my ribcage and all the way back to my spine. I had nice breasts, but no one saw them because when my shirt was off, I knew the only thing anyone would ever see was the scar.

And now, it'd be the only thing Jalen ever saw when he looked at me.

I grabbed the clothes in his hands and yanked them on as he apologized and asked questions and swore that he hadn't meant to invade my privacy. I ignored all of it and avoided even looking at him. It wasn't his fault. He hadn't done anything wrong. But I couldn't even reassure him because I had to focus on breathing, putting one foot in front of the other.

Running away. Because that's what I did when things went wrong. I ran.

TWENTY-TWO

I DROVE BACK TO MY APARTMENT IN A COMPLETE DAZE, barely remembering any of the trip itself. In the back of my head, I knew I'd been lucky not to hurt myself or someone else, but the majority of my brain was caught up with the horror of Jalen having seen my scar.

Jenna explained that she hadn't gotten plastic surgery on any of her scars because, to her, the scars meant she'd survived. Mine was the result of surviving when I shouldn't have, but it was also a reminder of everything I'd lost, of the life I could never get back.

I'd managed to put all of that behind me, and while my life was far from perfect, I'd been as happy as I'd ever expected to be. Then I'd taken Jalen's case, and everything had gone to hell. I'd been willing to accept things being complicated when I planned on being an FBI agent, but once that dream was no longer a possibility, I'd been great with settling for something simple.

I closed the apartment door behind me, finally letting out the choking sob that had been clawing at my throat from the moment Jalen walked into the bathroom. I sank to the floor next to the door and pressed my face against my knees.

It was too much happening all at once. The physical strain of being beaten up, not sleeping or eating right, and rough sex combined with the adrenaline from all of that plus the investigation itself. My emotions had been subjected to as much of a rollercoaster ride as the rest of me, and that had been the last straw.

"Rona?"

My name was followed by a knock on the door.

"Go away, Jalen." My voice was muffled, but I didn't doubt he could hear me. "The case is done."

"I'm not here about the damn case, and you know it."

He sounded annoyed, and that was enough to get me to raise my head. I wiped my cheeks and took a couple shaky breaths.

"We don't need to have the talk," I said, closing my eyes. "I get it. You can walk away without feeling guilty."

"What the hell are you talking about?" He slapped the door with his palm. "Do you really think I'm so shallow that I'd care about a scar?"

A stab of guilt cut through my self-pity. I was being unfair to him. He at least deserved to say his piece. Maybe hearing it would let me deal with things out of anger rather than this unbearable mixture of grief and longing.

I pushed myself to my feet and opened the door mid-knock. I stepped back and let him inside, not looking at him as he passed by.

"You said we could start over," he began. "I wanted to do this right. Talk to each other instead of jumping to conclusions."

"You're right," I admitted. "I shouldn't have run away."

"Why did you?" He closed the distance between us and hooked his finger under my chin, tipping my head back until I could meet his eyes. "Because of a scar? Do you honestly think I'd care about that?"

Sadness filled the small smile that curved my lips. "Even if you didn't mean to, it'd be on your mind, wanting to know what happened. Thinking about it every time you touch me. Something like that, people don't look past, no matter how good their intentions."

He grasped my chin to keep me from looking away and something fierce burned in his eyes. "I won't lie and say that I don't want to know the story, and I won't apologize because it's as much a part of you as your childhood, your adolescence. It's one of many things that all make up the amazing woman you are, so yes, I'd like to know. But I'm not going to push you. I'll only say that I'm here to listen if and when you're ready to tell me."

A small ray of hope bloomed inside me. "Are you sure you can handle that?"

He rested his palm on the side of my face as he wrapped one arm around my waist. "I'm not rushing us into anything. Right now, it's about us liking to spend time together."

"You mean we like fucking each other."

He laughed. "Definitely that." His thumb brushed against the corner of my mouth. "What do you say we give this a shot? Slow. No labels or expectations other than neither one of us hooking up with anyone else. We talk and ask questions, but if we don't feel comfortable answering, we let it go. Secrets are okay but lies aren't."

I thought for a moment, turning his words over and over in my mind. "Okay."

The hand on my cheek moved to cup the back of my head as he lowered his mouth to mine. The tip of his tongue traced the seam of my mouth as he pulled me flush against him. My nipples hardened into little points, and without my bra, they were on display for anyone who cared to look. It didn't matter that I was still sore from being with him only a couple hours ago. I wanted him again. Whatever this connection was between us, my appetite for him was proving to be insatiable.

He slid the hand on my waist down to my ass, squeezing as he kept our bodies pressed together. He was hard, and I knew if I took him in my hand right now, it would be so easy to have him inside me again. Zipper down. Pull him out. Pants down. One thrust, and he could take me right here against the wall, and all I'd do was beg for more.

Before any of that could translate from imagination to reality, my phone rang.

I reluctantly disentangled myself from Jalen and dug in my purse. The screen showed a number I didn't recognize, but with everything that had been going on recently, it was better to answer the phone and deal with a sales call than miss something important.

"Hello?"

"Hello. May I speak with Rona Quick?"

"This is she."

"My name is April, and I was asked to call you."

I froze. Had my father contacted someone to reach out to me and try to talk me out of testifying against him again? "Asked by who?"

"Adare Burkart. She's in the hospital."

TWENTY-THREE

THE NURSE HADN'T TOLD ME ANYTHING OTHER THAN the fact that my boss was in the hospital and was asking for me, but that had been enough to get my brain working overtime, thinking of all the possible things that could be wrong. I was no doctor, but even I could come up with plenty of reasons why she'd be in the hospital, and each one was worse than the last.

"Rona?" Jalen reached over and took my hand. "I know you're worried about Adare, but don't get caught up in trying to figure out what's going on. It'll just drive you crazy. We're only a few minutes away."

I nodded but didn't say anything. He was right, I knew, and I appreciated all he'd done for me since I'd gotten the call. Found me something appropriate to wear. He hadn't asked a question other than wanting to know which hospital, and that had been because he'd insisted on driving. Not that I'd protested much. Or at all. I wasn't safe to be on the road right then.

"I mean it, Rona." He squeezed my hand. "We're almost there."

"Thank you," I managed. "For everything."

"I'm not going to cut and run again," he said. "I promise."

Neither one of us spoke again until we reached the hospital. He pulled up in front of the doors and told me to go on in. He'd follow after he parked the car. Once I was inside, it didn't take me long to get the room information. She was up on the sixth floor, but I didn't realize what that meant until I made it to the elevator and saw the sign.

Oncology, sixth floor.

My stomach dropped, and all I could hear was the blood rushing in my ears. Cancer. She was here because of cancer.

Sure, there were kinds of cancer that didn't have as high mortality rates as others, and there was treatment, but my gut told me things weren't going to be that simple. This was bad. Really bad.

"Rona?" Jalen's arm slipped around my shoulders. "I got the room number. We can go now. Sixth floor...shit, Rona..."

His voice trailed off, and I knew he'd seen the same thing I had. His arm tightened around me, but he didn't say anything. Instead, he led me on to the elevator and pushed the right button. Less than a couple minutes later, we walked onto the sixth floor and down the hallway until we got to the right room.

I wanted to tell him that I could take it from here, that he didn't need to stay, but as I stood in the doorway of that room, I found that I couldn't send him away. Not yet.

"It's okay," he said quietly. "I won't go until you're ready."

I nodded.

"Rona."

Adare's voice was weaker than I'd ever heard it. I took a few steps into the room and my stomach twisted. She wasn't a big woman, but she'd been solid when I'd first met her. A former athlete, a woman who'd always done things on her own, for herself. I'd seen her a week ago, and she'd been fine.

Except...she hadn't been. Looking back, I could see the extra lines on her face. The weight loss I'd taken for a normal reaction to stress or being overworked. The numerous absences.

"Have a seat," she said. "There are some things I need to tell you."

I didn't want to hear what she had to say, but this wasn't about me. It was about her. What she needed.

"Mr. Larsen, would you go ask a nurse for some water?"

I felt Jalen looking at me, and I nodded. "I'll be back in a bit." His lips brushed the top of my head, and then he was gone.

I sat down, scooting the chair closer to the bed. She pushed herself up against the pillows, grimacing as she shifted. I would've told her not to strain herself, but I knew her better than that. No point in arguing with her about something she'd do anyway.

"When we first met, I told you that I didn't sugarcoat things, and that hasn't changed." She gave me a smile that didn't quite take the pain out of her eyes. "As I'm sure you figured out, I have cancer. Pancreatic. Terminal."

"Then why aren't you—"

"My chances weren't good from the first," she cut me off. "Any treatment would've maybe given me some extra weeks. A couple months if I was lucky. And they probably wouldn't have been great months. I decided that I wanted to leave things on my terms. Mostly good days, and then just a few bad ones."

She was dying. One of the few people I'd actually let get close to me since I lost Anton, and she was dying.

And soon, if I understood correctly.

"Why–" I croaked, then cleared my throat before I tried again. "Why didn't you tell me before?"

She raised an eyebrow. "Because I knew you wouldn't let me die in peace. You'd nag me into getting treatment and spoil all of my plans."

"Plans to end up here?" I gestured around her. The room wasn't bad, as far as hospital rooms went, but that was beside the point.

"Plans to go on with my normal life for as long as possible," she said. "Now, how have things been going with your cases? Mr. Larsen came in with you. Does that mean there's a break?"

"Adare, we don't need to talk about the cases."

"Yes, we do." Her expression sobered. "Burkart Investigations is my legacy, Rona. I want to know how it's been doing."

How was I supposed to say no to that?

The answer was, I couldn't.

Even though I would've preferred to talk about extending her life, I told her about the work I'd done on Jenna's case so far, and about everything that had happened with Jalen's case. Well, almost everything. She didn't need to know about the personal stuff.

"And that's all?" she asked when I finished. "No other reason that Mr. Larsen is out hunting down some water for me?" Her dark eyes sparkled.

"I don't know what it is," I answered honestly. "There's

something between us, but we haven't had time to really explore exactly what."

"He's very attractive."

I flushed. "Seriously? *That's* where the conversation is going now?"

She smiled, then sucked in a breath, pain creasing her face.

"Adare?" I stood up, reached for her, then stopped, not knowing what to do. "I'll get someone."

"No." She reached out a hand to stop me. "It's okay. It'll pass."

"Adare, please, let me help you."

She gestured for me to sit down. I didn't want to, but again, I knew better than to push her. I sat.

"I'm asking for your help," she said. "I have family, but I'm not close to them. My attorney has letters to send to them, explaining things. I won't be asking you to talk to them."

I leaned forward, my heart picking up speed just a bit. "But there is something you're asking of me."

"There is." Pain twisted her pretty features again, and I waited until it passed. "I've made all the arrangements for after I'm gone. What I want done. It's all written down, along with all of the receipts and contact information. Everything's been paid for."

This couldn't be real. She couldn't be talking about her death like it was nothing more than an event that needed planning.

"My will is there too, in the fireproof box in the bottom drawer of the far-right file cabinet in the office. The business is yours."

I shook my head. Waited for the words to make sense.

Then shook it again when they didn't. "What are you talking about?"

"Burkart Investigations. It's yours. When I interviewed you, I wasn't looking for an employee or even a partner. I wanted someone who could take over, who could keep things going after I was gone." She smiled at me. "I haven't known you long, but I feel like you'd take care of it better than anyone else."

I wanted to tell her that I couldn't do it. I couldn't be what she wanted me to be, *who* she wanted me to be. I'd tried to make my mother proud, and I'd fucked that up. I'd do the same with what Adare wanted of me. I'd let her down. Ruin everything she'd worked for, spent her life on.

"Six months," she said. "I only asked for six months in my will. After that, you can sell it, liquidate it, or whatever you want."

I stared at her, waiting for her to laugh and tell me this was all some terrible joke. But her gaze was steady as she waited for me to process it all.

"Okay," I finally agreed.

She smiled. "Was that so difficult?"

Before I could respond, Jalen appeared with a jug of water, grinning that charming grin of his. "I come bearing libations."

She looked at me. "Oh, he's a keeper."

I looked at him, and something in me twisted sharp and bright.

That's what I was afraid of.

TWENTY-FOUR

If anyone ever wondered how people could possibly sleep in those hellishly uncomfortable hospital chairs, the answer was simple. Spend more than thirty-six hours experiencing some extremely stressful shit, and most people would sleep like babies. It was more like passing out than sleeping, but it worked.

It was Sunday afternoon, and I hadn't left the hospital yet. I'd told Jalen to go home, but he said he'd stay with me that first night. Then we'd talk about what I needed to do so I could stay with Adare until the end. Which, according to her doctors, would be before the new week was done. With the amount of medication they were giving her, she'd sleep more and more until she stopped waking up.

"Excuse me, Miss Quick?" A woman in a gray suit came into the room. "I'm Mrs. Sheely, the head of the hospital. We're ready to move you and Miss Burkart."

"Move us?"

"To the private room Mr. Larsen arranged." She frowned. "He didn't tell you?"

"He must not have gotten around to it," I said with a tired smile. At some point, Jalen and I would need to talk about my issues with people helping me, but anything that made Adare more comfortable, I wouldn't turn away.

It was closing in on noon by the time we were settled into the small private room, and Jalen had left a few minutes ago to get me some real food. I fully intended to sneak some of my food to Adare if I could get her to eat it. He was also going to pick up some toiletries and clean clothes, so I wouldn't have to leave until...it was done, as well as my laptop and some books. He was taking care of everything without me even needing to ask him, and I knew it would come back to bite me in the ass, but I couldn't ask him to stop.

A part of me wished that he was here now though. Even the short move had been hard on Adare, and she'd been given some extra morphine. Now, she was asleep, the low, steady beeping of the heart monitor the only thing letting me know that she was still alive. Unfortunately, that beeping wasn't enough to keep my mind from going to the bad place it'd been edging around ever since I'd seen the word 'cancer.' I wasn't exactly a people person, but I would've liked some company right about now.

"Hey, Rona."

I turned at the soft voice coming from the doorway.

"Jenna?" She gave me an embarrassed smile, then flushed when I hugged her. "Thank you for coming. How'd you know?"

"Jalen." She stuck her hands in her pockets and glanced

over at Adare. "He called Rylan to talk and mentioned you might want some company for a couple hours this afternoon."

I shook my head. "He's taking care of so much."

"He's taking care of *you*," she said with a smile. "Take this from someone who didn't like being taken care of...let him do it."

I raised an eyebrow.

"I think I can safely say that you and I are a lot alike. When Rylan and I first met, we were working together, and I wasn't interested in a relationship. Neither was he. But we needed each other." She gave me a pointed look. "The two of you need each other."

I sighed and flopped back into my chair. "I've got so much on my plate right now, Jenna."

"I'm not saying marry the guy. Just let him take care of you."

I decided the best way to not have this discussion was to change the subject. "I got a break in the case I was working for Jalen."

"I heard." Her face lit up. "You stopped some pretty nasty guys and saved a bunch of girls. Agent Matthews told me that the trafficking ring you busted wasn't just selling sex slaves. They were also supplying slaves to sweatshops all over the south."

My smile was tired but genuine. "That's great."

"We'll have to work together soon. Take down some more dirt-bags."

"That sounds good," I said. "And I'll get back to your case soon."

She shook her head. "Don't worry about my case. I've waited years to meet my siblings. You take the time you need." She glanced toward Adare. "Being there for someone you love is more important than anything."

Having Jenna there did more than give me a distraction. She reminded me of the importance of Burkart Investigations, of the work we did. Sure, the majority of cases weren't life-changing, but some of them were, and that was worth consideration.

Jenna also reminded me that Adare and Jalen weren't the only people in the city with whom I had a connection. Jenna was already a friend, but the more time I spent with her, the closer to her I felt. I had a real chance to make a home here, and Adare's gift would go a long way to help me make it.

I looked at her again. When she next woke up, I'd tell her that I'd honor her wishes, and I'd do my best to make Burkart Investigations into everything she'd always wanted it to be. It would be a lasting legacy to the woman she was.

I just wished she'd be around for years to enjoy it. Short of a miracle, however, I knew that wouldn't happen.

"HEY."

I looked up from the book I'd been attempting to read for the past hour. The familiar face made me jump up from the chair. "Clay!"

He caught me in a hug. "I'm sorry about your friend."

"Thanks." I stepped away as I glanced over at where Adare was sleeping again.

She'd had a good of couple hours where she'd been able to talk to me, Jenna, and Jalen. Once Adare had drifted off again, Jenna had excused herself, telling me to call her anytime. Jalen had stayed until thirty minutes or so ago, but then left to get us food. I kept telling him that he could go home, and I'd call him if I needed him, but each time he just smiled and shook his head. He hadn't said it in so many words, but I knew he wasn't leaving for good until I did.

"How'd you know I was here?" I asked suddenly.

"From my partner, Agent Matthews. He told me about the girls you rescued, and I have to admit that I was more than a little annoyed that I had to find out about it from him. Then he told me that your friend was in the hospital." He reached out and squeezed my shoulder. "Is there anything I can do?"

I shook my head. "There's nothing anyone can do for her. Knowing you're here is enough for me."

"No matter what's happened between us, I'm always going to be here for you. You know that, right?"

I nodded. "I know. Thank you."

"Nice work, by the way," he said. "Saving those girls." He paused, then added, "You would've made a hell of an agent."

"Agent?" Jalen's voice came from behind me. "I thought you were an investigator." He stepped up next to me and held his hand out to Clay. "Hi. Jalen Larsen. We haven't officially met."

"Because the last time you saw me, you behaved like an ass?" Clay grinned to take some of the sting out of his words. He shook Jalen's hand, and I had no doubt that both of them were doing their best to break each other's knuckles.

"I did," Jalen admitted. "But I've apologized for it, and she's forgiven me."

"She's good like that," Clay said.

"She is." Jalen slid his arm around my waist and brushed

his lips against my temple. "But I'd still like to hear about this agent thing."

"Before I moved here, I was in school to be an FBI agent," I said honestly. "It didn't take." Okay, that was a little less honest, but that wasn't a conversation I was ready to have yet.

I could tell he wanted to know more, but he didn't push, and for that, I was grateful. I was doing okay now, but I wasn't sure how long that would be true for. If I was going to get through this, I preferred to do it with people I could count on.

TWENTY-FIVE

"It won't be long now," the nurse said as she pushed a button on the monitor, quieting the beeping that had been going slower and slower over the last hour.

I nodded but didn't look away from Adare. It was Tuesday afternoon, and she hadn't woken up since late last night. She'd told me on Sunday night that she'd signed a DNR months ago. No ventilators or CPR. When her breathing stopped, when her heart stopped, it would be over.

I tightened my grip on her hand, but I didn't expect a response. She hadn't squeezed back since the early hours of the morning. I didn't need the nurse to tell me it wouldn't be long. I could feel her slipping away.

The nurse stepped out, but I knew she wasn't going far. Once everything stopped, she'd come back. I wasn't alone though. Jalen was here. He'd moved a second chair over so that he was sitting close enough to touch, but not so close that he was hovering. If I needed him, all I had to do was ask.

Her hand was cold, and I rubbed her fingers even though

I knew it wouldn't actually help anything. No one could do anything now but be there when she went. It was something I hadn't had with my mom or with my uncle. Even though my relationship with Adare wasn't the same, I was grateful for the opportunity to be here, so she didn't have to go alone.

I watched her chest rise. Fall. A long beat. Rise again. Beat. Fall. Repeat. Repeat. Each pause was longer than the one before, and I knew it was preparing me for when the pause became more than just a pause. I started counting the beats. Two seconds more each time.

And then...nothing.

I didn't need to look at the monitor to know that the line had gone flat. I kept holding her hand even as the nurse came back. She moved around me, turning things off as she went.

"I'll give you some time," she said quietly. "Just let me know when you're ready."

I nodded, and she left. I kept holding her hand for a few minutes longer, letting it sink in that she was really gone. I'd seen enough dead bodies in my life to know what it looked like when the life inside was really gone, and when I looked at her face, I knew it was true. She'd gone peacefully, and now the lines in her face had been smoothed out, making her look more like the woman I'd first met a few months ago.

There were some calls to make, but none that needed to be done right this moment. She'd arranged for the hospital to call her attorney, and he'd make most of the calls himself. Everything else could wait until tomorrow.

I stood up so suddenly that I swayed on my feet. I reached out to grip the bed, but I didn't need to because a strong arm wrapped around me, supporting me.

"It's all right." Jalen's voice was low in my ear. "I've got you."

I leaned into him, too weary to do anything other than accept what he offered. When he asked if I wanted to go, I nodded. Adare didn't need me anymore. Not here, anyway. She needed me to take care of the few arrangements she'd left to me, and to run Burkart Investigations. For that, I needed to rest and heal...physically, mentally, and emotionally.

I DIDN'T REMEMBER FALLING asleep in the car, but I knew I must have because when I opened my eyes, I was in a bed. Not my bed, but still a bed rather than a chair. Something about the place seemed familiar, but I couldn't quite place it. My head was thick, and I suddenly became aware of an urgent need to pee.

I stumbled out of the bed and through an open door that luckily led to a bathroom. After I'd relieved myself, I washed my face as well as my hands, letting the cool water help clear away the cobwebs. It wasn't until I straightened and saw my reflection that I realized I wasn't wearing the same jeans and sweater that I had on when I'd left the hospital. I was in a pair of familiar-looking flannel pants and a massive sweatshirt.

"I thought I heard you up." Jalen came into the bathroom just as I was rinsing my mouth out with some mouthwash I'd found.

"What time is it?" I asked. My voice sounded rusty, which fit with the fact that my mouth had felt like I'd been sucking on dirt-flavored cotton for a while.

"Nearly two," he said as he leaned against the doorframe.

"Oh, um, okay." I rubbed my forehead. "I can call a cab to take me back to my place."

"You don't have to leave right away. Let's get some lunch, and we can talk things over."

"I don't want to put you out any more than I already have," I said. "You have to get up for work..." The rest of his words registered, and I blinked at him. "Lunch?"

"It's two in the afternoon," he clarified. "Wednesday afternoon."

I stared at him. "I've been asleep for nearly twenty hours?"

"More or less. You got up sometime around midnight to use the bathroom, but I'm not entirely sure you were really awake."

"How did I...?" I looked around, bewildered. "I kinda need you to fill me in here."

He held out his hand, and I took it, needing the physical touch as much as I needed him to ground me. As he led me back into the bedroom, and then into the hall, he said, "You were asleep before we got out of the hospital parking lot, and I didn't want you to be alone, so I brought you back here. I behaved myself, I promise."

I didn't ask who'd changed my clothes. There wasn't anyone else here. It should have bothered me, that he'd taken off my shirt – and my bra, I realized – but it didn't. It might bug me later, it might not, but at the moment, everything still had that vague numb feeling that things took on when they hadn't entirely settled.

"What about work?" I asked.

"The thing about owning the company, I can work from home as much as I want to. And I was smart and hired a good enough group of people to take care of business that I don't even need to do much of anything."

I followed him into the kitchen but pulled him to a stop before he could tell me to sit down. "You don't have to do this."

He looked down at me, his expression serious, but his eyes light. "I know, but I want to."

"Why?"

He kissed my forehead. "Because you need to let someone take care of you for once, and I'm taking the job."

"Don't you mean you're *applying* for the job?" I asked, hating the way my heart skipped at his words.

"No," he said easily as he released my hand. "Because that implies you have other possibilities, and I refuse to accept that."

His tone had a teasing note to it, but it didn't fool me for a minute. Unless I wanted to specifically tell him that I didn't want to be here, that I didn't want him taking care of me, he wasn't going anywhere.

It surprised me how much I liked that idea.

TWENTY-SIX

A FEW FLURRIES SWIRLED THROUGH THE CHILLED AIR, but the ground wasn't quite cold enough for it to stick. The officiant Adare had selected asked if we wanted to move things inside, but I said no. Nothing short of a natural disaster would get me to deviate from the plans she'd made. I owed it to her to see things done right.

As I took my place in the first row of chairs, I couldn't help wondering if she'd have been pleased with the turnout. Her attorney had contacted her family like she'd wanted him to, but none of them were here. She'd told me that she hadn't expected them to come, but in my mind, I'd thought she had to be wrong. Who would miss their own child's funeral? Or their siblings'?

There hadn't been a service for my mom, not with things having happened the way they did. Anton had only been twenty-seven then, and without any other family, it had all been on him.

It'd taken everything inside him just to deal with the

M. S. PARKER

aftermath of what happened as well as my injuries. He hadn't had the heart or strength to arrange anything. Some people might have been upset by it, but we hadn't stayed in Indiana long enough for me to find out. By the time I'd asked about the funeral, we'd been in Hell's Kitchen, and I'd been relieved to hear that I hadn't missed anything. He'd promised that if I ever wanted to do something, we would, but I'd known that a memorial would only bring back memories that were better off left where they were.

There weren't many people there, but Adare had wanted it that way. Over the years, she'd stayed friends with some of her past clients, and they were all here, but she hadn't wanted an open service. As the news had gotten out, however, waves of cards and flowers had come into the office. She hadn't been some big public figure or a wealthy supporter of various foundations, but she'd been genuine in who she was, and people had loved her.

Jalen took the seat next to me, immediately reaching for my hand. I'd never thought of myself as someone who needed a lot of physical contact. I didn't flinch away from it exactly, but it wasn't something I'd found myself gravitating toward. Jalen did it automatically with me though, offering comfort that I didn't even know I needed. Or, more accurately, that I didn't want to acknowledge that I needed.

"Adare Burkart was many things to many people." Tall and rail-thin, the officiant didn't look like he had enough strength in his wiry frame to produce such a deep bass voice. "I was blessed to be among those who called her a friend. When my late wife, Cecily, came home from Christmas shopping with a story about a woman who'd chased off a potential mugger, I knew I had to meet the fierce woman Cece had described."

Each person here had a story like that, I realized. None of them had known Adare as a child or a teenager. They'd all met her in one crazy way or another. People from every walk of life imaginable, all brought together by a single person.

She'd come to Fort Collins as a college student, which made the elderly criminal justice professor from Colorado State University the person here who'd known her the longest. I'd heard that story already. How a stubborn sophomore had wanted in his class so badly that she'd camped out in front of his classroom for an entire week before the semester had started.

The middle-aged redhead a few seats to my left had been the victim of a car-jacking twenty-three years ago. After Adare had found the car and given the police information that had led to the jacker's arrest, she'd asked Laura Briggs out on a date, and they'd stayed together for five years. When they'd ended their romantic relationship, they'd remained good enough friends for Adare to want her here.

Behind me was a family of three who'd been smuggled into the country by a coyote who'd then held the youngest brother hostage in order to force the other two to work as drug mules.

To their left was a couple who'd just celebrated their thirty-ninth wedding anniversary because Adare had gotten to the bottom of false infidelity rumors being spread by a business rival.

Sitting here now, I could see more clearly than ever the gift Adare had given me when she'd left Burkart Investigations to me. It wasn't simply a way to earn a living, a legacy in success. It was a way to build a family of my own choosing. A way to make a difference in people's lives that I wouldn't have been able to do even as an FBI agent. Not every 'bad guy' was going to cross the agency's radar. Not every case would deal with breaking the law.

And, sometimes, I might need to be the one doing the law-breaking.

When the words were all said, it was time for me to do my final job today. I stood, and Jalen stood with me. His hand on the small of my back reminded me that I had more than one reason to thank Adare. I smiled as I stooped to pick up a handful of dirt.

"I get it," I said quietly. "I get it now, and I promise, I'll do you proud."

One by one, each of the people whose lives she'd touched came forward to say their goodbyes. There'd be no mingling afterward. Adare's orders. Once it was done, it was done, and we were supposed to go live our lives.

A life that was a little poorer for her not being in it, but a life she'd believed in more than I'd realized before now.

This time, I took Jalen's hand and led the way back to his car, neither of us looking back.

TWENTY-SEVEN

"I DON'T WANT TO BE ALONE TONIGHT," I SAID AS JALEN walked me up to my door. Technically, the apartment above the office was mine now, but I couldn't bring myself to go inside yet. I'd get there, but not tonight. "If you're okay with that."

He followed me inside, tugging me to a stop even as he pushed the door closed behind us. He wrapped his arms around me, and I settled against his chest with a sigh.

"I'll stay with you as long as you want," he said. He kissed the top of my head and held me for a minute longer before letting me go. "Why don't you go sit down? Are you hungry? I'll get you something to eat."

As he walked toward the kitchen, something low in me clenched. I was hungry, but not for food. I needed something *more*. Intellectually, I knew that sex after a loss was natural, a whole affirmation of life thing, but I'd never really experienced it before now.

"I don't want to sit down," I said, "and I don't want food."

He turned around, a puzzled expression on his face. "Is something wrong?"

I shook my head. "Just thinking about what I really do want."

"What's that?"

My heart thudded against my ribcage, but I wasn't going to chicken out. I'd never done this before, but if I could do it with anyone, it was him.

His gaze followed my hands as I reached down and pulled my shirt over my head. He breathed out a curse, but I could barely hear him over the blood rushing in my ears. I reached behind me, numb fingers fumbling with the hooks in my bra. As it dropped to the floor, my chest tightened until I could barely breathe. A part of me couldn't believe I was actually doing this, but another part of me was glad I finally had the guts to do it.

He came toward me slowly, but I didn't see any disgust or revulsion on his face. If anything, he wore an expression that looked an awful lot like awe.

"Damn," he muttered.

For a moment, I thought he was commenting on the scar, and that would've still been better than anything I ever would have thought anyone would ever say about it. Then his fingers lightly traced across the tops of my breasts, and I realized what was actually holding his attention.

I flushed, heat flooding across my skin even as my nipples tightened into two hard little points. I'd touched myself, but it wasn't the same. I'd had men touch my breasts before, too, but always over clothes, and always worrying about whether or not they'd seen or touched my scar. But Jalen, he'd already seen it. And he didn't care about it. All he cared about was paying attention to my body.

I moaned as his fingers tweaked and rolled the sensitive flesh. Definitely not the same as touching myself. Fuck. I closed my eyes, and my head fell back. I'd never imagined that I was missing this much by limiting how someone could touch me, but this...

His tongue circled my breast, and my eyes snapped open. I grabbed the back of his head as he wrapped an arm around my waist. He held me steady, tracing wet patterns across my skin, then blowing cool air. My skin prickled, goosebumps spreading despite the heat coursing through me.

The hand on my back moved up my spine, then back down to the top of my ass. I was vaguely aware that he was touching the end of my scar, but he didn't say anything, and neither did I. He shoved his knee between my legs, using it to help keep me steady. When his lips closed around one throbbing nipple, I understood why.

With a hard pull of his mouth, he sent electricity straight from my nipple to clit, igniting everything between. I cursed, my body shifting without thought, the movement pushing his thigh up against me. I shivered at the pleasant friction, rocking my hips against him for more. He chuckled, the vibration against my nipple my new favorite sensation.

Until his teeth got involved.

The hand on my back guided my movements as I rubbed on him, and his teeth worried at my nipple, the combination exactly what I needed. I'd been wound tight for what seemed like years, pressure bubbling just below the surface.

"Come for me," Jalen said. He bit down, tugged, released. "Come for me, and I'll take you to bed."

My pussy clenched at his words. I wanted that. *Damn*, I wanted it. Wanted him. Inside me.

"Come, Rona." His voice had an edge to it. "I'm so fucking hard right now. I need you to come, and then I can fuck you."

Most men would've assumed I wanted to be comforted with something soft and sweet. Made love to. Not fucked. But he knew me well enough to know that what I needed right now, what would actually comfort me, was fucking.

He shoved his hand under the back of my skirt, palming my ass, squeezing it. "Don't *think* about it. *Do* it."

He moved his mouth to the side of my breast and bit down – hard – and worried at the skin, sucked on it. Marked it. He pushed his leg more firmly against my core, and I whimpered.

"J..." I panted. "J...J..."

And there it was.

"Yes!" I cried out as I rode his leg, taking myself up and over the edge. I fell forward, trusting him to catch me, and he did. He held me there, helping me eke out every drop of pleasure until I finally went limp in his arms.

He straightened, scooping me up in his arms as he went. I almost protested that I wasn't the best size to be carried, but then I remembered that he'd done it before. I half-expected him to toss me onto the bed, but he set me down gently instead, sliding off my skirt and panties as he went.

"You soaked clean through these." He grinned down at me as he deposited my clothes in the nearby hamper. After taking off his shirt, he moved on to his pants. "Damn, babe. My pants are wet too."

I shrugged, enjoying the way his eyes dropped to my breasts when I moved. "You told me to come."

He nodded. "I did." He glanced behind him at a red silk scarf hanging over the edge of a chair, then looked down at me. "Do you trust me?"

"Yes." The answer came before I was even aware of what it would be.

I watched as he walked over to my scarf, and the sight of all those muscles bunching and flexing sent a rush of arousal through me, sharp and sweet. His face was gorgeous enough, but that body...damn.

When he turned back around, scarf in hand, I felt silly for not having realized already what he wanted to do.

He leaned over me, his eyes locking with mine until the scarf hid him from sight. A shiver of anticipation, tinged with fear of the unknown, went down my spine. Not seeing him at all when he could see all of me took a lot more trust than I'd realized.

The bed dipped under me as he moved. "Spread your legs and put your arms above your head."

I stretched my arms up, my fingertips brushing against my pillows. No matter where things went between the two of us, tonight would always be special to me. He was giving me something no one had ever been able to give me before, not even Clay.

"No thinking, no analyzing. Just feel."

He grasped my ankle, slid his hand up my leg. I could feel his gaze on me as he hooked one leg over his hip, hitching it up high and opening me to him even more fully. He paused a moment, then surged forward, burying himself inside me with one thrust.

My back arched, mouth opening. He groaned, a wordless sound wrung out of him. We froze like that for several beats, locked together in an intimate embrace. Then, when I couldn't bear it a second longer, he rotated his hips, rocked back and forth, as if he was gauging my responses.

When I pushed up against him, he leaned closer, my thigh muscles burning as my knee pressed closer to my chest. He drove into me with single-minded purpose, each stroke taking me to my limit. The words we said didn't make much sense, a jumble of curses and endearments and compliments, each one's sole purpose to express how much we were enjoying the feel of our bodies coming together, the sensations of skin on skin – complete for the first time.

I could have lied to myself that the only reason this felt so much different from other times I'd fucked was because I wasn't constantly aware of my scar or because I wasn't wearing a shirt, or even because of the blindfold, but I knew better. I knew it was because of Jalen, because of the trust between us, the connection we had. And when we came, him first and me seconds later, that connection only grew stronger.

TWENTY-EIGHT

"IT'S OKAY," I SAID SOFTLY AS I TURNED MY HEAD TO look up at Jalen. The hair on his chest scratched my cheek, but I couldn't find it in me to mind. I was more content here than I'd ever been with another person.

"What's okay?" he asked as he brushed some hair back from my forehead.

I rolled back a bit, exposing as much of the scar as possible. "Touch. Ask. Satisfy your curiosity."

"I don't need to know," he said, "not if you don't want to tell me."

He meant it, and that assured me I could do it. That I *needed* to do it.

I picked up the hand on his stomach and placed it between my breasts. That was all the encouragement he needed. He traced the scar with his fingers, followed the rough edges down and around to my spine.

"Who hurt you?" The anger in the question meant as

much to me as the question itself. Not *what happened* but *who hurt you.*

"I grew up in Carmel, Indiana," I began, returning to my place against his side. I traced patterns on his skin as I told my story. "The court transcripts were sealed, so not many people outside of that town know what I'm going to tell you, and even there, not all the details got out."

He ran his hand up and down my arm but didn't interrupt.

"I was an only child with a normal childhood, up until I was twelve anyway. My dad had an accident at work, and it messed with his brain. He changed from my funny, hard-working father into someone who flew off the handle at the slightest thing. He was scary, but my mom and I, we still loved him."

His stomach muscles tensed under my hand, as if he guessed how bad the next bit was going to be. I doubted his guesses had even gotten close to what I was about to tell him.

"About a year after it happened, I was in my room, putting away clothes, and they started yelling. They'd been yelling a lot since he'd gotten hurt. I didn't realize anything was really wrong until something crashed." I swallowed hard. I needed to talk about it the same way I had on the stand. "My mom screamed. I went downstairs, and there was blood everywhere. My mom was dead. No question or doubt. Before I could really even process it, my dad grabbed me, threw me up against the wall. He had this knife from our kitchen, and it was covered with blood."

"Shit." The word was more breath against my hair than sound.

I touched the spot where the knife had first gone in. "The

tip got stuck in my sternum. He had to work it back and forth before he could get it to move again, which is how a shallow cut left that much of a scar."

"Rona." His voice cracked.

"I don't have to tell you the path the knife took." I gestured to the scar. "It wasn't deep enough to hit anything too important, but it got all twisted, like you can see. Some of it was him. Some of it was me trying to get away. Which I didn't. I ended up on the floor, and he must've thought I was dead. I passed out, but not for long. I still don't know how I managed to get up and get to a phone. I called 911 and then heard the kids next door screaming."

"Fuck, babe." His arms tightened around me.

"He killed the housekeeper and the babysitter. She was a couple years older than me." I pushed back the memory of finding Darcy with her throat cut. "Dad had the kids trapped in the bathroom. He was screaming, pounding on the door. I could see it breaking and tried to shove him away. He pushed me down, and I saw he'd dropped the knife. I stabbed his leg, and he kicked me in the head."

I shivered, and Jalen pulled my blanket up around me.

"You don't have to tell me anything else," he said. "Get some sleep. I'm here."

I nodded. That was pretty much all there was to tell anyway. What had come after was about what could be expected. Recovery. The trial. Moving away so I'd never have to hear about it.

Jalen was right. I'd rehashed enough of my past tonight. I was safe here. He'd keep the nightmares away.

TWENTY-NINE

"I'VE GOT YOU."

The words struck panic hard and deep. I gasped for air, and it was like someone had built a fire in my lungs. Each breath burned, but to not breathe was worse. Black spots danced in my vision, blocking out the owner of the voice.

I didn't need to see him to know who he was. I knew his voice, the feel of him. He'd made me feel safe, and now he was stripping that away from me, replacing it with fear.

It was the ultimate betrayal, to have the person I trusted the most let me down. He said he had me, but I knew he didn't. He was walking away, lies still falling from his lips, smile still on his face.

I tried to call out to him, to tell him that I still needed him, but my voice caught in my throat. Once he disappeared, I'd never see him again. I'd be left with the new him. This cold, angry creature who knew only violence and pain. He'd hurt me and like doing it because that's all I would be to him. An outlet for all the misery he held inside.

*How could things have changed so fast? I didn't under-
stand. Was I truly this naïve that I'd believe he meant
anything he said? He'd broken my heart, and he would take
my life. It'd be easy to do. I was only a shell of a person, more
fragile than anyone realized.*

*Was that what had finally turned him away? Seeing me
for who I was? A coward who couldn't stop him. A child who
couldn't save her mother. A woman who failed at everything
she did. A friend who couldn't save her mentor. A lover who
couldn't keep him.*

*Two hims. Two men. Both betrayers. Both heart-breakers.
Men of lies and violence. I'd given my heart to one from birth,
and he'd protected it...until he tried to destroy it. I'd given my
heart to another, and he crushed it.*

"I've got you."

*I heard the sarcasm now, dripping from every word. The
laughter underneath the promise. A mockery.*

"I've got you."

He let me go.

"I've got you."

He tried to kill me.

"I've got you."

He hurt me, and he'd do it again.

"I've got you."

No one ever stayed. No one...

I jerked awake, disorientation lasting only a few seconds
before I registered where I was. My apartment. Home. Jalen
had brought me back here after the funeral. I remembered
now. We'd had sex, and I told him my story. He'd held me
while I'd fallen asleep.

No wonder I'd had such a confusing nightmare, mixing

past and present, my father and Jalen. It was actually more surprising that I hadn't experienced more nightmares over the past week. Stress usually brought them on more often.

It was morning, and the light in my room was enough for me to see that I was alone in bed. I could hear Jalen in the shower though, and the sound helped me relax. He hadn't snuck out.

I pulled the blankets more tightly around me and gave in to the desire to snuggle back down into the bed. I wasn't self-indulgent often, and today seemed like a good enough day to give it a shot. Besides, it was Saturday. I hadn't done much in the way of work this week, but I didn't see the point of opening up before Monday, especially since all the work fell to me now.

I was still lazing about when Jalen came into the bedroom. His hair was still wet, and he wore only the dress slacks he'd worn to the funeral. He looked...lickable. I pushed myself into a sitting position, prepared to enjoy the view. He bent over to pick up his shirt, then visibly startled when he saw me.

"You're awake."

"I'm thinking a lazy Saturday might be just what the doctor ordered," I said with a smile. "We can make brunch out of whatever I have in my kitchen and just veg out. Watch some TV. I'm sure you're as exhausted as I am. I really appreciated you being there–"

It wasn't until just then that I realized he wasn't looking at me. In fact, he was looking everywhere *but* at me. I might've written it off as him dressing, but his cheeks were flushed. I frowned.

"Is something wrong?"

"Don't you feel like we went from zero to ninety in ten seconds flat?" he asked.

I tucked my blanket more tightly under my arms, suddenly self-conscious once more. "What do you mean?"

"This." He gestured around us. "We went from complete strangers to staying over at each other's places and talking about all this deep, personal stuff."

"I've got you."

The voice from my dream echoed in my head as my body went cold.

I could have reminded him that he'd been the one to initiate our first kiss. That I hadn't exactly had to twist his arm to get him to have sex with me. I could've reminded him of how he'd later regretted the asinine way he'd behaved, both that night and when he'd found Clay here. There were dozens of other instances I could have brought up, times when he'd clearly been the one taking the lead or insisting that he stay with me when I told him to go home.

I didn't say any of that though. I didn't say anything. I couldn't. All I could do was stare at him.

"I'm not saying I don't like you. Things are just going too fast. We need to take a step back."

A step back.

I wasn't an idiot. I knew that was what people said when they wanted to leave but didn't want to look like the bad guy. I'd just lost someone close to me and told him about the worst thing that had ever happened to me. If he flat-out broke things off, he'd be the worst sort of asshole. A step back meant that he wasn't abandoning me. Just taking some time to think. Getting some air.

Retreating like a fucking coward.

"I've got you."

"You understand, don't you?" He still couldn't meet my eyes. "It's been a lot to deal with."

I swallowed a bitter laugh. I wasn't going to give him the satisfaction of knowing how deep he was cutting. I also wasn't going to tell him it was okay. It was fucking far from okay. I managed a tight nod.

"Do you want me to walk you out?"

I barely recognized my voice.

"No." He shook his head, relief flooding his features. "Thanks."

I didn't know if he was thanking me for the offer or for what he thought was agreement on my part. I didn't care either. I just wanted him gone.

"I've got you."

The front door closed, and the sound echoed back through my apartment, confirming that I was alone. If I believed in fate or destiny or any of that shit, I might've thought my dream was prophetic.

Instead, I saw it for what it was. A reminder of the truth I'd let myself forget.

Men left.

"I've got you."

For years, I'd blamed my mom for what happened, for not leaving my father and getting us out of that situation, but the one thing I'd never felt toward her was abandonment. She hadn't chosen to leave me. If anything, it had been her loyalty that had gotten her killed.

No, my father had been the one who'd taken her away, and he'd taken himself away too. Sure, he'd had that accident at work, and it'd changed him, but I'd heard enough about what happened to know that the accident had been his own fault. He hadn't been paying attention to his work, and it'd bitten him in the ass. He might not have exactly chosen to walk away, but it'd been his poor choices that had put him in the position to get hurt.

"*I've got you.*"

Anton hadn't chosen to leave either, but he'd known how dangerous people could be, and he hadn't taken enough precautions to keep himself safe.

"*I've got you.*"

Clay...Clay had never left me. I'd run away from him, but he'd looked for me. Without Anton around, he could have ignored me. There were so many times I'd done things that should have driven him away, but *he'd* stayed.

"*I've got you.*"

I threw off the covers and got out of bed. I knew exactly what I needed to do and where I needed to go. The first thing I needed was a shower. Then, I'd pack a bag.

THIRTY

I WAS STANDING IN FRONT OF THE DOOR, MY HAND STILL in the air after knocking, when I realized that I probably should have called to let him know that I was coming. The only reason I even knew his address was that he'd put it into my phone when he first came to Fort Collins to see me. He'd told me that it meant I wouldn't have any excuse to not see him at some point.

I had a feeling he hadn't meant showing up on his doorstep on a Saturday morning, but the moment Clay opened the door, I knew I'd made the right choice by coming here.

"Rona? What's wrong?"

"Can I come in?" My voice was even, but I knew I was on borrowed time for that.

"Yes, of course." He stepped aside, and I walked past.

I didn't go far though because he grabbed me with one arm and pushed the door closed with the other. He crushed me against his chest, and I could finally breathe. I pressed my face against his chest, the soft material of his sweatshirt as familiar as his scent.

"Give me a minute," I mumbled, "and I'll fill you in."

He smoothed his hand over my hair. "Take your time. I'm in no rush."

I stayed where I was until my body finally relaxed. Every inch of me ached from the tension I'd been carrying over the past few hours, but I felt better just being with Clay. Even if I wasn't attracted to him anymore, he was the closest thing to family I had left.

"Let's sit," he said when I stepped back. "You can tell me why you're here, and I can tell you why I'd been planning on driving down to see you later today."

I looked up at him as I made my way over to the sofa. The apartment was nice, but definitely a bachelor pad. I wasn't about to start critiquing his décor or housekeeping. I wasn't his girlfriend.

"You go first," I said as he disappeared into what I assumed was the kitchen.

He came back with two beers and handed me one.

"A little early for that, isn't it?"

His expression was grim as he sat next to me. "My news alone is worth at least one beer. Judging by the way you came here, I'm guessing yours is the same."

"Shit, that's ominous."

He raised an eyebrow as he took a long swallow, and I followed suit. I'd been crazy to think that I could ever actually have a nice, boring life.

"Everything for your dad's new trial got rolling this weekend," he said. "I ran interference with the DA's office, let them know what was going on, and they did what they could without you, but you need to be back in Indiana Monday morning."

Fuck. Yeah, that was worth alcohol. I took a long drink, but even the buzz I was getting from drinking on an empty stomach wasn't helping.

"I can take care of travel plans," he continued, "and you'll have police protection waiting for you when you get there."

I nodded, still trying to wrap my head around what he was saying. I hadn't forgotten about the trial, not really, but things with Adare had pushed it out of my mind. In a way, it hadn't actually felt real before, more like it was part of one of my nightmares. Now, though, hearing Clay talk about travel and police protection, it all became a hell of a lot more real.

"Are you going?" I asked. "To the trial?"

He looked at me for a moment. "Do you want me to be there?"

I could've told him no, that I could do it on my own. I'd done so much on my own already. I could stay with him for a bit now, get my head back together, then take care of things myself. I didn't need him to be there with me.

But I wanted him there.

The first time I testified, I'd been a teenager – a young one at that – and I'd had my uncle there for support. I was an adult now, but it would be nice to have a friendly face in the courtroom when I took the stand. Especially since my gut was telling me that my father's new defense attorney wasn't going to be as...*polite* as the last one.

It was one thing to come after a woman in her twenties with no visible injuries – and no way in hell would I wear something revealing enough to show my scar – and something else altogether to come after a teenage girl, still bandaged and hurting. There had been no way to downplay what my father had done to me, and no way to question what I'd seen without risking upsetting me and making the jury sympathize with me. This time, my memories could be called into question without risking much in the way of pity. Not only were they the memories of an adolescence, they were from nearly a decade ago.

I hadn't seen my father since the day he'd been sentenced, and the thought of it had my stomach in knots. That, plus testifying again, made me want to have someone I could look to, someone I could lean on.

"I would," I said quietly. "But only if it won't be a problem for work. I don't want to inconvenience you."

He rolled his eyes. "I've got some vacation time stored up. I'll take it."

We settled back against the couch, sipping our beer while lost in our own thoughts. It was a comfortable silence, and it made me long for what we had been. I didn't want him, not even like I had before, but it would be easy to turn to him for physical comfort. He was as gorgeous as ever, and I knew he could do things to my body that would make me forget for a while. He wouldn't argue with me, and it would be so easy to lean over and kiss him.

But it wouldn't be fair to either of us.

I'd be wishing he was someone else, and he'd be wondering if things between us were changing again.

I wouldn't do that to him.

He broke the silence. "Will you be okay with me hearing everything at the trial?"

"You've already read the file."

"I did," he agreed, "but I don't want you to be up on the

stand, talking about the things that your dad did, then look at me and get thrown off because it's stuff you haven't talked to me about."

"Trust me, it wouldn't make me feel any better if I'd told you everything myself." I glowered at my beer, then finished it off.

"Shit." He looked over at me. "Did you tell him? Jalen Larsen?"

I nodded. "Let's just say I overestimated him."

"Bastard," he growled.

I looked over at him, all of the emotion I'd been trying to hold down twisting inside me. "I can't completely blame him. It's a lot to take." I plucked at the front of my shirt. "Not to mention what Daddy Frankenstein did to my torso."

"Bullshit," Clay said. "Don't you dare put the blame anywhere other than right where it belongs. On Jalen."

I shrugged. "You might not say that if you saw it."

"Then show me."

The words hung there, stark and terrifying. Clay had seen the medical reports, the pictures from the first trial. He knew what my father had done to me, but he'd never seen the end result. And now, even though he knew I'd trusted a virtual stranger before I'd trusted him, he wasn't angry. He was offering me the chance to have someone react the way Jalen *should* have reacted.

What the hell.

I sat forward, closed my eyes, and lifted my shirt. Clay let out a low whistle, and the knot in my stomach loosened. I opened my eyes and lowered my shirt. Clay's eyes met mine, and they burned.

"If your father gets off, I'll kill him."

I smiled, tears pricking at the corners of my eyes. "Thank you. And I'm sorry for not showing you before."

He gave a dismissive wave. "It's okay. I get it. Things with us have always been...unconventional."

"Thank you," I said again. "It means a lot to me that I can count on you."

He put his arm around me and pulled me against him. "No matter what happens, Rona, you can always count on me."

I flopped back on the couch and leaned against him. "If that's the case, would it be okay if I crashed here today? I just can't face going back to my apartment tonight."

"Of course," he said. "You've always got a place in my bed." I smacked his stomach, and he grinned at me. "My guest bedroom, I mean."

I laughed and remembered why being with Clay felt so good. Coming here had been the right thing to do.

THIRTY-ONE

I just wanted to lay down and go to sleep. Never wake up. Everything hurt and going to sleep would stop it. All I wanted was for the pain to stop. But I had things to do.

Miles to go.

Miles to go.

My feet dragged as I staggered outside. Forward. Forward. Toward the sounds. Push back the dark. Keep moving.

Miles to go.

Miles to go.

Through the front door. Foot sliding on bloody tile. Down on one knee next to a body. Mrs. Khaled. She had the kids bring me cookies when Dad was hurt last year. Eyes open. Staring at nothing.

Up. Up.

Push through the pain.

Hold the skin together. Keep insides in. Ignore blood oozing between fingers.

Squishing between toes.

Miles to go.

Miles to go.

Bang.

Bang.

Bang.

Knock on wood.

Break wood.

Screaming. Crying. Screaming.

Miles to go.

Miles to go.

Toes bump. Don't look down. Keep moving. Don't look down.

Can't stop myself.

Blonde hair-soaked red. Gaping smile. Wider. Wider. No teeth. Just gushes of scarlet and crimson.

Hot liquid gushing through fingers.

Not hers.

Mine.

Hers cooling. Thickening.

Miles to go.

Miles to go.

Leave her behind. Can't help her. Must keep going. Help them. Help them.

Miles to go.

Miles to–

"No!" The word caught in my throat, and I choked on it.

"Miss are you, all right?" The elderly man next to me hit the button to call for a flight attendant.

I nodded, grabbing for my bottle of water. I drained it,

then focused on slowing my breathing. Hyperventilating was the last thing I needed right now.

"Bad dream," I gasped out.

That was a bit of an understatement. I'd been having nightmares two, three times a night since Clay told me I needed to come back. The flight from Denver to Indianapolis wasn't a long one, and I hadn't planned to sleep, but I hadn't been able to help myself. I was exhausted.

I rubbed my hand over my face and sighed as I leaned back in my seat. The little screen on the back of the seat in front of me showed our progress. We were about to start our descent.

"Everything okay here?" A smiling flight attendant appeared.

"I had a bad dream," I said with a tight smile. "It's okay. I'm good now."

"Are you sure?" she asked. "You don't need anything?"

I shook my head. "We're not too far out, are we?"

"No. Not much longer now."

"I used to have nightmares," my seatmate said as the flight attendant walked away. "Every other night for months, I used to have the same nightmare. Jellyfish. I got stung by one when I was five, and when I watched that damn lost fish movie with my granddaughter, it all came back to me, and the nightmares started again. Damn things chasing me. Yelling *squishy* at me and throwing blobs of jelly."

I stared at him. What the hell? Was I still sleeping?

He kept going until the seatbelt sign flashed on, and then he started giving me statistics about plane crashes versus car crashes and even threw in the occasional train wreck. Just for the fun of it.

Normally, listening to all of that while in a plane would freak me out, but I had to admit, it kept the butterflies in my stomach to a manageable level. It would've been easier if Clay had been with me, but when he'd called in his vacation time, Agent Matthews had asked him to come in for a couple hours. Which meant that Clay was coming in on a later flight, and I was returning home alone.

I hadn't been back here since Anton and I had boarded the plane two days after my dad was sentenced. I'd never planned on coming back. Hell, I'd planned on giving Indiana, Illinois, and Ohio a wide berth for the rest of my life.

As we headed for the runway, I gripped the arms of my chair, my knuckles turning white. My seatmate assumed the issue was with the landing, but a part of me was actually hoping that we crashed so I didn't have to walk through those glass doors and into that city.

I'd do it, of course. Go to the courthouse. Testify. I'd relive all of it if it meant keeping my father in prison.

But it didn't stop me from wishing I didn't have to do any of it.

"Dammit, Clay," I whispered.

I immediately felt guilty. He was coming as a favor to me. He was taking time off work to do it. I wasn't going to be a bitch and whine because he had to take a few hours to straighten some things out before he came out here to hold my hand.

"It's okay, sweetie." My seatmate reached over and patted my hand. "We've landed safe."

I gave him a tight smile and concentrated on not screaming. I had a feeling I was going to be doing that a lot over the next few days.

I really hoped Clay had warned my police escort, because if I slipped and started freaking out, it would be fucking embarrassing.

Just one more thing to look forward to.

THIRTY-TWO

I LIKED THE ADA TRYING THIS CASE. NO BULLSHIT. Straight to the point. She'd called me when the trial had broken for lunch and asked me to come to her office at five. We'd eaten takeout, and she'd gone over things with me.

Vijay Castellanos was ambitious, that much was clear, but she didn't let it get in the way of her humanity. She still believed in the system and her part in all of it.

When she'd been satisfied that I wasn't going to freeze up or go back on what I'd originally told the police and then the jury, she'd told me to go back to the hotel and get some sleep. I was going to be called first thing in the morning, and she needed me well-rested.

I didn't bother to tell her that I hadn't been well-rested in a long time. I was half-tempted to ask the cop outside to run to the store and get me something to help me sleep, but I knew those things left me groggy for at least an hour after I woke up. I needed to be sharp first thing tomorrow. Vijay had confirmed what I'd already been thinking. The protections

I'd been given last time wouldn't be there for me this time. The defense was going to hammer me about accuracy, as well as question my motives, my relationship with my parents, and anything else they could do to put my testimony in doubt.

Basically, a fun time for all.

Those were just a few of the many things I was thinking about while I stretched out on the bed, wearing my favorite flannel pajamas, and flicking through channels. I wasn't actually looking for anything to watch, but I had a feeling I'd go crazy if I turned it off. I didn't need silence right now.

Someone knocked on the door. "Miss Quick?"

I sighed and climbed off the bed. A quick look through the peephole revealed the cop who'd been standing outside my door, now looking thoroughly annoyed.

"Yes?"

"You have a visitor," he said. "I told him to go away, but he's quite insistent that you'll want to see him."

I smiled as I pulled back the security bar at the top of my door. Clay had texted a couple hours ago to say his flight was delayed and he didn't know what time he'd get in, but he must've found another flight. That was good. I didn't think I could handle being alone tonight.

"I'm glad you could get–" It wasn't Clay. My entire body stiffened. "Jalen. What are you doing here?"

I didn't even try to be polite. Not even when I saw how awful he looked.

Dark circles under bloodshot eyes. Face pale and drawn. Clothes rumpled, as if he'd slept in them.

I couldn't help the satisfaction that came with the realization that he'd been miserable this weekend, and I really didn't want to. I didn't consider myself a vindictive person by nature, but the way he'd handled things had been immature and hurtful.

"May I come in?"

I crossed my arms, glaring at him. "I don't think you're really in a position to be asking that."

"You're right. I deserve that." He glanced behind him at the annoyed police officer. "But I think your bodyguard here would feel better if you weren't standing in the doorway."

"And I'm safer with you in my room?" I asked. I slathered on the sarcasm. "Because you'd never hurt me."

He flinched, more color draining from his face. "I deserved that."

"Damn right you do."

I looked over Jalen's shoulder at the clearly uncomfortable cop. His job was to protect me and make sure I showed up at the courthouse tomorrow. He wasn't here to listen to whatever bullshit Jalen was selling.

"Come in." I stepped aside. When the officer took a step forward, I said to him, "It's okay. He doesn't have anything to do with the case. Just an ex who feels guilty for being a shit."

I closed the door and walked back over to my bed. I sat on the edge and pointed at the stuffed armchair against the wall. Jalen sat, elbows on knees as he leaned forward. I could feel the nervous energy rolling off him, and it set my teeth on edge.

"How'd you know where I was?"

He flushed, rubbing the back of his neck. "I went to talk to Rylan, and when Jenna was chewing me out for what I did, she accidentally let it slip that you'd gone back home for something. I made a few calls."

"Nice to know that anyone can find me if they have

enough money."

"I'm sorry," he blurted out. "I was an idiot."

He paused, looking at me like he either expected a reaction or a reassurance. I wasn't going to give him either. "Go on."

"I don't blame you if you never want to see me again. I lost any right to be a part of your life when I let my fear get the best of me." He took a deep breath and raised his eyes to meet mine. "And that's what it was. Nothing pure and simple about it. I've never felt this way about anyone before, not even Elise."

"You don't think I was scared too? It's not an excuse. You don't hurt people you care about."

"You're right," he agreed. "It's not okay that I took my insecurities out on you. I should have been upfront about what I was feeling."

I'd thought that hearing him apologize would give me some sort of closure, but it was too soon. The wounds were too raw.

He cleared his throat and went on, "Aside from Jenna and Rylan, I don't know anyone with a functional relationship. Look at Elise and me. We crashed and burned. Epically. My parents split when I was eight. When my dad got married a few years later, he shut me out. My mom's current relationship is the longest one she's had since my dad, and I doubt it'll last much longer."

I opened my mouth to tell him that his cynicism wasn't my problem, but he raised a hand, and I waited. The faster he got it all said, the faster he'd leave.

"I thought I loved Elise, and maybe I did at some point, but our relationship was so chaotic and emotional that it nearly destroyed me. When I caught her cheating, I promised myself I'd never let myself get in that deep with anyone ever again." The corner of his mouth tipped up, but there wasn't any real humor in the half-smile. "People say that if you want to make God laugh, tell him your plans. He must've been laughing his ass off when I met you."

I gritted my teeth and reminded myself that it didn't matter what he said. It mattered what he did, and his actions had proven more than once that he had no idea what it meant to care about someone.

Except...he'd taken care of me at the hospital. I hadn't asked him to do anything. He'd just done it.

"I'm not perfect, Rona, and I'm not going to lie and say that I'll never fuck up again, but if you give me another chance, I'll do my damnedest to make sure you don't regret it." He took a deep breath, and then added, "I'm falling in love with you."

His confession hit me like a fist. Why did he have to say that? Why couldn't he have just apologized, made excuses for his behavior, then left? Why did he have to make things so hard?

"How can I trust you?" The words came out as a whispered question rather than the strong accusation I'd meant it to be.

"I'll do whatever it takes, give you as much time and space as you need. I'll move heaven and earth if it means never breaking a promise to you. I'll understand if you don't think I'm worth the risk, but I'm begging you to give me a chance."

I didn't remind him that I'd already given him a second chance. That he'd fucked things up before, and we hadn't known each other that long. The problem was, I couldn't write off the bad behavior as being who he was any more than I could excuse the bad because of the good. People weren't saints or sinners. We were all complex beings, made up of millions of components.

"And there's something else. My divorce is going through and will be final soon. I gave Elise what she wanted, and she signed the papers. I'll be free soon. Completely free and finally ready to move forward."

I stared at him. For me. He did it for me, I knew.

"I'll go now." He stood. "Thank you for listening."

He was at the door before I told him to stop. "You want a chance to prove yourself?"

"More than anything."

I released a long breath. "Then stay with me tonight."

"Of course. I—"

I held up a hand. "No kissing or sex," I clarified, wanting to be completely honest. "This isn't a romantic getaway. I have to testify tomorrow, and I don't want to be alone tonight. Clay was supposed to be here, but his flight was delayed. Can you just be my friend?"

Jalen's eyes blazed with something so intense that it made my chest hurt. "I'll be your friend as long as you'll have me. And I'll prove to you that you can count on me."

It was a great declaration, but I didn't know how much I believed it. Or how much I even wanted to. He wasn't the only one who struggled with being cynical. I wanted to hope for the best, but I didn't have the energy to do that right now. If he could get me through this, maybe I'd take the risk again, but I pushed those thoughts out of my head.

First, I had to get through tonight.

THIRTY-THREE

"Say it."

Clay gave me a quick sideways look, then turned his attention back to the road. "Say what?"

I rolled my eyes. "Come on, Clay, I know you're dying to tell me what you think. How this is a bad idea, and I'm making bad choices because of this shit with my dad coming back up again."

"I never said any of that," he pointed out. "You're the one saying it."

"Because you're thinking it," I said. "I saw the look on your face when you saw Jalen."

"In your hotel room," Clay said. "Let's not forget that I saw him in your hotel room. A room that has only one bed."

"He came to apologize, and I asked him to stay." I refused to regret my decision. He hadn't tried anything, not even when I'd asked him to sleep on the bed next to me. When I woke from a nightmare-free sleep, I'd been curled up against his side, but he hadn't tried anything then either.

"Do you think that's a good idea?" Clay asked carefully. "After what happened with him before?"

"We had a good talk," I said. "And he asked me to give him a second chance." I put my hand on Clay's shoulder. "I've got my eyes wide open, and he knows he's got a lot of work to do to earn my trust back."

"I just don't want to see you get hurt."

"I know." I squeezed his shoulder before dropping my hand. "And I appreciate that. If he fucks up again, I promise to let you beat him up."

"I'm going to hold you to that."

As we pulled up to the courthouse, my mouth went dry, and the butterflies in my stomach took flight again. I could do this.

Clay reached over and squeezed my hand. "You've got this."

Sure I did.

"ONE FINAL QUESTION, MISS QUICK," Vijay said. "The events you're testifying to occurred nearly ten years ago. How can you be certain that your memories are accurate?"

Some prosecutors might have shied away from the question, hoping that the defense wouldn't bring it up, but Vijay had told me that she preferred to cut off some of the more basic arguments the defense would make by asking the questions herself. This was the big one.

"My high school history teacher once said that there are certain events that people always remember exactly where they were when those things happened. Pearl Harbor. The moon landing. JFK's assassination. September eleventh." I looked over at the jury. "What happened that day wasn't a small event within a series of things that happened around me. It wasn't seeing a glimpse of a stranger. What he – what my father did – destroyed my entire world. That's not the sort of thing that's easily forgotten."

"Thank you." Vijay looked at the judge. "No further questions for this witness, Your Honor."

The judge glanced at his watch. "It's nearly noon. Let's break for lunch and be back here at twelve-thirty. Forty minutes should be enough. Once again, let me instruct the jury that you're not to discuss the case with anyone, that includes speaking with witnesses or lawyers."

I let out a shaky breath before I stood. My knees felt like jelly, but I stayed standing, so I counted it a win.

"Great job," Vijay said as she walked with me back to the witness room. "I'll order us some food, and we can go over the most likely question the defense will ask."

I nodded in agreement as I made my way around the room. My muscles were tight from the combination of stress and sitting for the past two and a half hours. Vijay had been brutal, but not cruel, as she'd taken me through everything from my father's accident to waking up in the hospital the day after the murders. There'd been no glossing over things, no shortening them like I'd done for Jalen. She'd already gone through different parts of the timeline with other witnesses and shown pictures of the crime scene. I was the crux of the case though, tying the facts to emotions.

I reminded myself I was halfway done and sat down next to Vijay as we waited for our food to arrive. I wasn't really hungry, but the last thing I wanted to do was pass out on the stand, so when my chicken salad arrived, I forced myself to eat it.

Before I'd had enough time to completely decompress, it was time to go back. The judge and jury entered. I went back to the stand and was reminded that I was still under oath. I took my seat and braced myself.

Malcolm McCloud was every negative stereotype of a defense attorney to the rich. Vijay had told me that his clients weren't usually wealthy though. He hadn't been able to make enough of a name for himself to generate the sort of clientele he needed for the lifestyle he wanted. She suspected he planned to use this case to make a name for himself as an attorney who'd do anything to win. Including tearing me apart on the stand.

"Miss Quick," he paused, then tilted his head as if something had just occurred to him. "That's not actually your name, is it? Not the name you were born with. You go by Rona Quick, but your real name is Rona Elizabeth Jacobe."

"Is there a question here, Your Honor?" Vijay asked.

"I'll rephrase," he said with a smarmy smile. "What names were you given by your parents, when you were born?"

"Rona Elizabeth Jacobe."

"Why did you change it?"

Vijay had warned me that the first thing McCloud would do would be to try to get under my skin and make me come across as a hostile witness, which meant that no matter how inane I found his questions, I couldn't lash out.

"Two reasons," I said evenly. "It made things easier to have the same last name as my Uncle Anton, and I had no desire to be connected to the man who'd killed my mother and two other women, and who tried to kill me."

"Because you hate your father."

Vijay stood. "He's testifying, Your Honor."

"Mr. McCloud, stick with questions."

He smiled at the judge. "Of course, Your Honor." He looked back at me. "Do you hate your father, Miss Jacobe?"

I clenched my jaw.

"Your Honor, please ask Mr. McCloud to address the witness by her legal name."

"Mr. McCloud..."

He held up a hand. "Sorry, Your Honor." He gave me an expectant look.

"My feelings about my father are...conflicted," I answered honestly.

"But one of those feelings is hate, is it not?" He adjusted his tie. "In fact, for a year before the tragic deaths of your mother, Annabeth Khaled, and Darcy Fitzsimmons, the two of you were constantly at odds. You got into trouble, and he laid down the law, and you hated him for it."

"Your Honor..."

"If you don't have a question to ask, Mr. McCloud–"

"I do, Your Honor." His eyes narrowed as he focused in on me. "Did you hate both of your parents, Miss Jac-sorry, Miss Quick? Didn't you have a real motive to want them out of your life?"

Okay, I hadn't seen this line of questioning coming. Getting me angry, discrediting my memories, those made sense. Him accusing me of the murders? *That* was crazy.

"I was thirteen," I said. "I argued with my parents, but I didn't want them dead."

"Not even after they refused to let you go to the Carlisle pool party the previous week?"

I frowned. "You think I killed...you think I'd commit *murder* over a pool party?"

"Wouldn't you?" He walked back to his table and picked up a picture. "Defense exhibit four, Your Honor." He handed it to me. "What's shown in that picture?"

My stomach flipped. "My diary from when I was a kid."

"Would you read the highlighted portion?"

"Your Honor, we received no notice of this evidence." Vijay was on her feet again, her cheeks flushed.

"The diary was in the original evidence boxes," McCloud said. "Ms. Castellanos has had it available to her for nearly ten years."

"He's not offering the diary," Vijay countered. "Just a picture, which *wasn't* included in the original evidence. There's no way to authenticate that the pages in the photo actually belong to Miss Quick."

"Miss Quick's word should be enough for verification, Your Honor."

"You're calling her credibility into question and want to use a credible testimony from her to do it?"

"She has a point, Mr. McCloud. Are you willing to allow verification by submitting the entire diary as evidence?"

I pressed my hand against my stomach and prayed that McCloud wouldn't want to risk it. The entry in the picture had been written in anger. Taken as only a few lines highlighted on one particular page, it could be pretty damning. But if they allowed in the diary, there would be plenty of other entries where I talked about how much I loved my family. Still, no one would want their childhood tantrums and crushes made a part of the public record.

"I'll withdraw the photo," McCloud said.

"Let's get back to it then," the judge said. "Do you have additional questions for this witness?"

"I do, Your Honor." He was smiling again. "Miss Quick, let's talk about your feelings toward Darcy Fitzsimmons."

WHEN I LIVED in Hell's Kitchen with Anton, one of our neighbors was this wizened old woman who talked in all sorts of odd phrases. One that she'd often said after a long day was that she felt like a washrag that had been used, rung out, and hung to dry. I'd never really understood what she meant, but as I stepped off the witness stand hours later, I finally got it.

"We'll reconvene tomorrow with the defense's first witness." The judge banged his gavel.

"You were great," Vijay said. "Go back to the hotel and get some sleep. The defense only has a couple witnesses, and after the way he came at you, I'm thinking his entire plan is to present as many other possible suspects as he can and get the jury to believe that makes reasonable doubt."

"Do you think it'll work?" I asked, my voice raspy. I needed something to drink.

"Not a chance," Vijay said. "I think Mr. McCloud thinks more highly of his skills as a lawyer than he should. This is his first big case. He's only done parking tickets and misdemeanors before. He probably oversold himself to your dad without even looking at the case."

I hoped she was right. People could believe some pretty crazy shit.

Clay waited just outside the courtroom, immediately engulfing me in a huge hug. "You did an amazing job."

"Thanks," I said as I took a step back. I appreciated the hug, but there was another set of arms I wanted around me.

"How are you doing?" Jalen came from my right, hesitating only a moment before hugging me. He'd been careful with how often he'd touched me today.

"Okay," I said. "Glad it's over."

"If you don't want to come for the rest, it's fine." Vijay looked from Clay to Jalen and then back to me. "It's okay for it to be too much. Lean on your friends, but don't feel like you need to come in. I'll keep you in the loop."

"I can't even think about tomorrow," I said honestly. "I just want to get back to the hotel and go to sleep."

"I've got a car out front," Clay said.

Jalen reached for my hand. "I can take her."

Clay's eyes dropped to where my fingers were laced between Jalen's. "I'm not sure I trust you to do it."

"Whether you trust me or not doesn't matter," Jalen said. "It's Rona's decision."

"After what you did?" Clay's voice held an edge as he took a step toward Jalen.

"Stop." I didn't say the word loudly, but both men stopped where they were and looked at me. "Clay, thank you for everything. You have been the best friend I could've asked for, and I don't want anything about our friendship to change."

"But?"

"But Jalen and I aren't...*friends*. We're...something else, and we need to spend time together if I'm ever going to figure out if I can trust him again."

Clay studied us both for a moment before nodding. "All right. I'll head back to the hotel. I'll be right down the hall if you need me."

"Thank you." I kissed his cheek.

"I'm going to hold you to what we talked about before," he said before he walked away.

"What did you talk about before?" Jalen was trying to sound nonchalant, but it wasn't working.

"I told him that if you hurt me again, he could beat the shit out of you."

Jalen stood still for a moment, then nodded. "Okay then." He gestured with our joined hands. "Should we go?"

We didn't talk on the way back to the hotel, and I was grateful for it. I didn't need conversation right now. Being able to lean my head on his shoulder and close my eyes, knowing that I didn't need to worry about anything, that was all I needed. He saw to all of it.

A new officer was waiting outside my door, and he gave us both a smile as we went inside. I appreciated the security, but now that Jalen was here, I wasn't sure I needed it anymore. My father wasn't some mob boss or one of those serial killers who had all sorts of crazy followers. It was just him. There wasn't really any need for protection.

It wasn't until I'd seen him this morning that I realized how scared I'd been about seeing him again. Anger, I'd admitted and accepted. Fear, *that* had surprised me. But then they'd led him in, and everything had vanished. Anger. Fear. I'd looked at him, and all I felt was pity.

He'd looked...old. Much older than I would've imagined.

His hair was thin and scraggly, unable to cover the scar that ran from the middle of his skull to just in front of his ear. As much a souvenir of his accident as his personality change. His skin was sallow and hung on him, almost as ill-fitting as his orange jumpsuit. But it was his eyes that were the worst. Blue like mine but looking nothing like mine. They moved constantly, looking at everyone and everything with the same flat hatred.

There was nothing left of the father I'd loved as a child.

"Rona?" Jalen touched my arm, bringing me back to the present. "You're worn out. Why don't you go get a shower, and I'll order us some food? Anything specific you want?"

I shook my head. He was right. I was worn out. Beyond it, actually. "Thank you." I put my hand on his shoulder and stretched up to brush my lips across his.

It was barely a kiss. Nothing like what we'd shared in the past. But it was a start.

His eyes lit up, and he started to lower his head for another kiss. I put my fingers on his lips, stopping him.

"I'm not ready for sex, not yet." I slid my hand to his cheek, the stubble rasping against my palm. "But I want to be there. I want to trust you again, want this to work. When I say stop, you stop."

His answer was to cover my mouth with his. His lips were gentle, moving with mine as I leaned into him. His body was firm and familiar, exactly what I needed to feel safe.

I really hoped he meant everything he'd said since he got here, because I didn't know if my heart could handle being broken again.

THIRTY-FOUR

The next two days were awful.

McCloud brought in Daniella and Clark Snowe, now sixteen and nineteen, and twisted everything they remembered into support of my father's defense. They'd both been in tears by the time their testimonies had been done.

Then he'd called Willis Jacobe himself.

My father hadn't testified in the first trial. His lawyer'd had a hard time keeping my dad quiet in the courtroom. There would've been no telling what he would've said or done. Or that had been what everyone had assumed.

Now, I wondered if it'd been because he hadn't wanted people thinking my father was crazy and wondering why that hadn't been the defense's position all along.

I'd listened in horror as he'd described what 'actually' happened. How my mother had told him that she was pregnant with another man's child, that she was leaving us. He'd left to deal with the pain of her infidelity and to think about what to do next. When he came back, he'd found my mother dead, and me in the neighbors' house with their kids locked in the bathroom and two more bodies on the floor. He never came out and said that I'd done it, but the implication was there.

And that had been the entire point. To create the 'reasonable' doubt that the jury needed to find him not guilty.

Closing arguments happened yesterday after lunch, and then the jury had been sent out to start deliberations. I wasn't sure which was worse, listening to my father lie about my mother and what he did or waiting to see if twelve strangers were still able to see the truth.

Even with Jalen at my side, I'd barely slept last night, and now, I kept pacing in the little alcove where we waited to hear if the jury had a verdict yet. If they didn't come back today, I'd go nuts. Plain and simple. I couldn't handle waiting an entire weekend to find out what they decided. The only thing worse than waiting would be if they couldn't decide at all.

I stopped, rubbing my temples. "Please don't let it be a hung jury," I mumbled.

"Rona?" Jalen put his hands on my shoulders. His thumbs dug into my shoulders, kneading the knots there.

I moaned, dropping my head forward. He leaned closer, letting me feel the heat of his body, a physical reminder that he'd been with me, here, through all of it. The feel of him sent a wave of warmth through me.

He pitched his voice low so only I could hear him. "I love hearing you moan like that."

I closed my eyes. Jalen had been amazing these last couple days. He'd never once pushed for anything more physical than comforting touches. He held me when we slept, and inevitably, he'd get hard, but he never took advantage of me. He'd been exactly what I needed.

"Rona." Vijay appeared. "The jury's back."

Jalen reached down and took my hand as Clay stepped beside me. The two men had settled into what felt like an uneasy truce. Clay was waiting for Jalen to screw up again, and Jalen didn't quite believe that all Clay wanted was friendship. I didn't bother trying to set either of them straight. Only time would prove what was true. Fortunately, they weren't asking me to choose sides. If they ever did that, both of them would lose.

The three of us made our way back to the courtroom, sitting down behind Vijay's table. My stomach twisted in knots, and I squeezed Jalen's hand until he winced.

"Sorry," I whispered, loosening my grip.

"It's okay," he said with a smile. "I get it."

My father entered and took his place next to his lawyer. The bailiff entered and called us all to order. The judge and jury came in, the tension in the room shifting as they did. While re-trying this case wasn't exactly headlining nation-ally, it was big enough in our area that everyone was waiting to see what happened.

Everyone, including the families of my father's other victims. I hadn't been able to even look at them. They didn't blame me, I knew. They'd all been there the first time we'd done this dance, and they knew what my father had done to me. They knew how much I'd tried to stop him.

But I hadn't been able to do enough.

Maybe that was why I'd felt so much responsibility back then. And still felt it today. It was my way of making amends. At least as best as I could.

"I understand you've reached a verdict," the judge said as the first juror stood.

"We have, Your Honor."

"On the first count, in the murder of Dana Jacobe, how do you find the defendant?"

"Guilty."

Everyone let out a breath.

"On the second count, in the murder of Annabeth Khaled, how do you find the defendant?"

"Guilty."

The dark-haired woman sitting on the other side of Clay let out a strangled sob. She was Mrs. Khaled's daughter, Gwen. She'd gotten married last year.

"On the third count, in the murder of Darcy Fitzsimmons, how do you find the defendant?"

"Guilty."

Darcy's mom started to cry, and Mr. Fitzsimmons put one arm around her.

"On the fourth count, in the attempted murder of Rona Quick, how do you find the defendant?"

"Guilty."

Clay put his hand on my shoulder, and Jalen squeezed my hand. It was done. The lesser charges that had been a part of the first case hadn't been made part of the appeal in order to streamline things. Those didn't matter. He'd been found guilty of the four counts that mattered. He'd spend the rest of his life in prison, where he belonged.

Most people would think that I'd be happy right then, but all I really felt was a sense of relief. It was over. I could go back to Colorado without any unfinished business here. My past was completely behind me, and I could move on.

Starting with my relationship with Jalen.

―――――――――

JALEN WAS STRETCHED out on the bed when I got out of the shower. He hadn't asked why I'd felt the need to take one when it was still early and all we'd done after court was get something to eat, and I didn't offer an explanation. Part of it was almost symbolic, a way of cleansing myself of the past, but another part was the need for some solitude while I figured out exactly how I wanted to approach things with Jalen.

By the time I finished, I decided that straightforward would be the best approach. Which was why I was now standing next to the bed, my towel wrapped around me, my stomach in knots.

"Thank you for everything you've done this week."

Jalen turned to look at me, his eyes widening when he saw what I wasn't wearing. He pushed himself up on his elbows but didn't say a word.

"And I'm sorry. I'm not saying what you did before was okay, but it was wrong of me to expect you to accept everything with a smile. I should have made it clear that it was okay if you needed time to adjust."

He shook his head. "What you went through–"

"Is in the past," I interrupted. "And that's where I want to keep it. No more looking back at what we did or said. We've made our apologies, and I don't want to dwell on any of it. I think we have something amazing here, and I don't want to lose it because I held on to something I should have let go."

He moved across the bed until he was kneeling in front of me. "I don't want to lose you either."

I let the towel drop, heat flushing my skin as Jalen devoured me with his gaze.

"Are you sure?"

I could hear the need in his voice, see it on his face, but he'd proven this week that he could put my needs above his own. If I told him that I didn't want him to touch me, he wouldn't.

"I'm sure," I said as I reached out. I carefully unbuttoned his shirt, surprised that my hands were steady. "No more lies or half-truths. I want us to be honest with each other about who we are and what we want. I want us to be able to trust each other with everything."

He caught my hands as I finished the last button. "I want that too." He raised my hands to his lips and kissed my knuckles. "I will probably fuck up again. You can pretty much count on it. But I will try every day to be the man you deserve."

I leaned forward and brushed my lips across his. "That right there is more important than a false promise of perfection."

He smiled at me. "Does that mean I get a reward?"

I smiled back as I pushed his shirt off his shoulders. "I think one can be arranged."

My hands moved across his broad shoulders and down his arms, his muscles firm under my palms. Back up again and then across to his chest. I went slower this time, exploring each dip and curve. Just enough hair to show that he didn't wax or shave, but not so much that it took away from the work of art that was his body. I could see the definition of muscle in his pecs, his abs, but he wasn't so cut that it looked unnatural. He'd been blessed with good genes and took care of himself, but not so fanatically that he obsessed over working out. Some women might like the bulging muscles and veiny arms, but in my mind, Jalen's body was perfection.

I scraped a nail across a nipple, and it tightened. I did it to the other one, and Jalen muttered a curse. I smiled and ran my fingers down his abs to the dark hair below his bellybutton. I loved how men's bodies, with their v-grooves and their happy trails, blatantly pointed to the body part they prized the most.

I leaned forward and used my tongue to trace circles around one nipple, then the other. My hands were busy undoing his pants when he put his hand on the back of my head, applying pressure until I realized what he wanted. I worked over the sensitive skin with tongue and teeth, biting harder and harder until his entire body jerked.

"Fuck, Rona," he groaned.

His hand tightened in my hair, pulling on it until I released his nipple with a wet sound. His mouth slammed into mine, and he wrapped his free arm around me, crushing me against his chest. I gasped, and he took advantage of my parted lips to invade my mouth, his tongue tangling with mine. He didn't say a word, but I could feel his possessiveness in the way he held my body against his, the way his lips and teeth bruised my mouth.

My nipples hardened as his chest hair scratched the sensitive skin, and I moaned, nails digging into his hips as I tried to pull him closer. I growled in frustration as his pants got in the way.

"You're wearing too many clothes," I protested as I pulled away.

He tried to grab me, but I'd refocused my attention on getting him naked as quickly as possible. I finished unzipping him and grabbed the waistband of his pants and underwear, yanking them both down to his knees. I ran my hands up his thighs, then back around to his ass. Damn, I loved his ass. One of my neighbors in Hell's Kitchen used to say that someone's ass was, "So tight I could bounce a quarter off it." I wasn't sure that was actually possible, but if it could've been on anyone's ass, it'd be his.

Then there was his cock. Thick enough that when he was hard, I couldn't wrap my fingers around it. Over average in length, but not too long. Some women might like that their man hit their cervix with every stroke, but not me. In theory, if the conditions were just right, it would spark off a whole other sort of orgasm, but I wasn't exactly itching to try. He could make me come hard enough to see spots without that particular maneuver.

I put my hand on his chest and pushed. He let himself fall backward, and I wasted no time removing his pants the rest of the way. Now that he was completely and wonderfully naked, I climbed up onto the bed as well. He watched me as I moved up his body until I was straddling his thighs. I kept my eyes locked on his as I grasped his cock and held it in place. I lifted up, maneuvering myself bit by bit until I was able to place the tip of him at my entrance.

I was wet enough that the head slipped right into me, but the rest had to be done at a much slower pace. I wasn't nearly ready enough.

"You're too fucking tight," he said, gritting his teeth. "Like a fucking vice."

I dug my nails into his stomach as I dropped another inch. "Fuck, J! Fuck! Dammit!"

"Does that help?" he asked, a strangled laugh escaping.

I glared at him. "You're not exactly small, asshole."

He grinned and slid his hands up the backs of my thighs to my ass. I sucked in a breath as one finger slipped between my cheeks. He rubbed the tip of his finger against the puckered muscle but didn't try to push inside.

"One day, I'm going to discover how it feels to be inside your ass."

He sounded so sure of himself that I almost nodded in agreement before common sense clicked in, and I thought about what it might feel like to have Jalen's huge cock trying to fit into that virgin territory.

"You can barely fit in my pussy," I said breathlessly. He was half-way inside now, and my body felt like it was being split in half.

Oral sex would've made this a hell of a lot easier.

"Have you ever done it before?"

I shook my head and started to reach down to play with my clit. He grabbed my hand, stopping me, and then replaced my hand with his.

"I can make you want it," he said, his finger making firm circles over my asshole as his other fingers played with my clit.

"How?" I grunted as I took another inch.

"I'd have you lay on your stomach, and I'd start with my tongue. Get you nice and wet." My muscles fluttered as he sank a little lower, and he cursed before continuing, "Have you ever been rimmed before?"

I shook my head. I'd never even considered it.

"I'll show you how it's done. Lick you open, then slide a finger inside. Just one to start with, but it'll feel huge at first. I'll go slow, letting you get used to it as I work in spit and lube."

The fingers on my clit moved faster, rubbing back and forth, then in a circle, and he watched my face with an intensity that made me shiver.

"When you've just gotten used to one finger, I'll push a second one in, twisting and stretching. It'll burn, giving you little twinges of sharper pain, but I'll start working your clit then."

His fingers pressed down on my clit, sending a rush of liquid over his cock, allowing me to slip lower on him until only an inch remained. If I hadn't taken all of him before, I might've doubted that I could now.

"Good girl," he murmured as I gasped and squirmed on top of him. His fingers were doing amazing things to my clit, and my pussy felt impossibly full in this position. "Do you think I'll be able to make you ready with just two fingers, or should I plan to use a third?"

My head swam. We'd fit together fine before, and I knew it was just the difference of position and preparation making it more difficult this time, but just because he fit in my pussy didn't mean he could fit everywhere. Could my ass really take him? I cursed as I fell the last bit, his cock lodged completely inside me.

"I think I'll need a third finger." His voice was rough. "Maybe you'll ask for even more."

More?

I opened my eyes to find him watching me.

"Maybe you'll want more than two fingers, or even three," he said again. "But three would be enough to make sure I didn't hurt you but still keep you nice and tight."

I splayed my hands out on his stomach and moved back and forth with deliberation, adjusting to the new position and how it changed the way he moved inside me. He put his hands on my hips, fingers flexing, but not pushing me to go at his pace. For the moment, he was letting me have control.

I rose up on my knees, keeping my eyes on his face as I sank back down. I swiveled my hips, leaning forward enough for the base of him to rub against my clit. Over and over I repeated the motions. Up. Down. Around. Up. Down. Around.

"You have no idea how big of a turn-on it is to watch you like this." He slid his hands up my sides and around to cup my breasts. He pushed them together, then let them fall back to their natural position. His hands moved across my torso, fingers tracing my scar. "Does it bother you?"

"What?" A familiar tightness was starting low in my belly.

"Me touching your scar. Does it bother you?"

I shook my head. "You don't act like it disgusts you."

He sat up, wrapping his arms around me. He lowered his head, pressing his lips between my breasts so that he was kissing the place where the scar began. "It doesn't. It's a part of who you are."

I linked my fingers behind his neck, taking advantage of the new position to move faster. I used my grip for leverage and leaned back, working my hips up and down. He put a hand on the small of my back, giving me extra support. Sweat glistened on my skin, and the only sounds in the room were of our ragged breathing and the slap of flesh on flesh as our bodies came together again and again.

His free hand moved to one of my breasts, covering it. He squeezed, and I shivered. He pinched my nipple, and I moaned. Each extra little jolt fed the fire burning deep in my belly, pushing me toward the point where it would finally consume me.

It didn't matter that we'd only slept together a couple of times or that we hadn't known each other that long. He knew exactly what I needed, even more than I did myself.

As I leaned farther back, his mouth replaced his hand. He took my nipple between his lips, worrying at it with his teeth. Light pressure, then increasing it more and more until the pressure became a pain, and I cried out. He licked along the scar between my breasts, then up over the soft skin until he arrived at my other nipple.

"J, please, please, please, please," I begged. My movements were frantic now, little jerks of my hips as I desperately sought release. Breaths came in ragged sobs, and I squeezed my eyes closed, every cell straining toward climax.

"You can do it." He wrapped his fingers around the back of my neck. "Make yourself come. Come on my cock."

Fuck.

"That's it, baby. Use my cock to get yourself off." His voice had taken on this gravelly tone that made me even wetter. "Let me see those tits bounce. Fuck, you're gorgeous. Let me see you come. You're so fucking hot when you come."

I shuddered, my muscles quivering as everything inside me tensed.

"Dammit!" he growled. "Keep squeezing my cock like that and I won't last much longer."

"Come with me," I begged. "I want to feel you come inside me while I'm coming."

I practically threw myself forward, grabbing at his shoulders as I ground down on him, my throbbing clit sending sparks of painful pleasure through me until I finally came with a wordless cry. He gripped me tight, body twitching against mine as he followed, emptying himself inside me.

We still had work to do on this relationship and returning to Fort Collins tomorrow wouldn't make things any easier, but we were in this together, and I believed we could make it. Still, I was glad we'd have the night here in our little bubble, far away from the outside world.

THIRTY-FIVE

H<small>E BROUGHT HIS HAND DOWN ON MY ASS WITH A</small> resounding smack, and I moaned in pleasure even as the pain spread out from where my skin burned. My ass had to be a bright shade of red by now, and I knew sitting after this was going to be an issue, but at least I worked a job where I didn't need to be behind a desk all the time.

"You have the best ass," Jalen said as he smoothed his hand over the burning flesh, the gentle touch the perfect balance to the sharp slap he'd given seconds ago.

"Yours isn't bad either," I said, my breathing heavy and sharp. "Does that mean I get to spank you next?"

He chuckled and smacked the other side of my ass before sliding his hand down between my legs. I gave a small yelp as he shoved two fingers inside me, and he laughed again.

"Always wet for me, aren't you?" He twisted his fingers, and I pushed back against his hand. His free hand smoothed up my spine and then back down again before he slapped my ass once more. "What do you think we should do about that?"

"Fuck me," I begged. "Fuck me, please."

He pulled his fingers out and buried himself inside me with one thrust. I cried out, coming again as he bottomed out. Even as I shook with the force of my orgasm, he pounded into me, not giving me the slightest respite.

We'd gotten back a few hours ago, thanks to his private jet, and he'd taken me to his place after asking if I wanted to go to my apartment. We'd barely made it through the door before we were stripping off our clothes. This was round two, and he'd already made me come three times. My entire body was on the edge, primed for another climax, and I knew he'd give it to me.

Every stroke hit me deep, hard enough to be painful, or at least they would have been if I hadn't been flooded with endorphins. I'd feel it tomorrow for sure – probably sooner – but right now, all I felt was good. Amazing, actually. Like every cell in my body was vibrating, full of ecstasy, just waiting to be released.

"Damn, I love you like this." He slammed into me hard enough to make me gasp. "Ass in the air, those firm tits of yours jiggling."

He reached beneath me to squeeze both of my breasts, then rolled my nipples between his fingers. I whimpered, the already tender flesh sending pain shooting through me. He'd been pinching, biting, and sucking on my nipples from the beginning, and they were excruciatingly sensitive at the moment.

"I've been a little rough on you, baby." He slid his hand across my stomach to slip a finger over my clit. I shuddered, tightening around Jalen until he cursed. "Or maybe not rough enough."

A moment later, I felt his finger pressing against my asshole. My eyelids fluttered as he pushed just the tip past the ring of muscle. The burn that would have made me gasp instead made me cry out as I came again. And again. One orgasm rolled into another until he finished with a loud groan.

The two of us collapsed onto the bed, a tangle of sweaty, trembling limbs. I knew we'd sleep now, exhausted enough that I knew we'd both go under soon. We'd need to get up eventually, but right now, I was content where I was. We'd doze, then do what was necessary when we woke again.

Tomorrow was a new day, a new start. My past was gone. Jalen and I had worked out things between us. Clay and I were friends again. I had a job I enjoyed and one I was good at. One that would allow me to help people the way I'd always wanted. I'd keep Burkart Investigations going and grow it into something that would have made Adare proud. And I'd offer my services to Jenna when she and the FBI worked on human trafficking cases.

I'd be a part of making the world better, making my mother proud of me.

And I'd have a life with Jalen.

I was feeling more optimistic about life than I ever had before.

It was time to start living.

THE END

The New Pleasures series continues in *Played by Him*. Turn the page for a free preview.

PREVIEW: PLAYED BY HIM

ONE

I STUDIED MY REFLECTION IN THE MIRROR, A STRANGE feeling of self-consciousness attached to the happiness I'd been feeling ever since we'd arrived back in Fort Collins, Colorado. It wasn't really about my appearance. I was used to being self-conscious about that, wondering if my scar was showing, if the shirt I was wearing was long enough to cover everything when I moved, if the neck was high enough. Now, when I looked in the mirror and saw the familiar ash blonde hair and china blue eyes, I wondered if people saw beyond that, if they could see the way I felt. Even though I knew it was silly, I felt like I should be glowing or something.

I'd had moments of happiness with Clay as a friend and as a lover. Moments with Uncle Anton where I'd forgotten that I should have had a different path. My life since my mother's death hadn't been all doom and gloom, but it hadn't been like this either. It wasn't about perfect circumstances or not being sad over Adare's death. It was about letting myself see a positive future, and with Jalen, with this life I had begun to build here, I could see it.

I turned away from the mirror and headed back into the office. I'd spent the last couple hours organizing and sorting through things. It had been less than two weeks since Adare's death and I hadn't exactly taken the time to go through Adare's things. Even when she'd been dying, she'd kept up with the bills, with the clients, and when I found the envelope with my name on it, I knew why.

I walked back over to the desk and sat in the chair. The envelope sat on the top of the desk and I stared at it, trying to work up the courage to open it.

This was how I knew I was really happy. Even the grief at losing Adare wasn't the sharp, debilitating agony that I'd known in the past. I missed her, and that wasn't going to go away anytime soon, but I'd known her well enough to know that she wanted me to be happy.

I let out a slow breath, picked up the envelope and opened it.

Rona,

I'm guessing, right now, you're pretty pissed at me for not telling you I was sick. I'm sorry about that. I'm sure we had this discussion at some point, and this letter isn't to go over it all again. It's to reassure you that you can do this. I wouldn't have left Burkart Investigations to you if I didn't have faith that you could make it into everything I always wanted it to be. Don't doubt yourself.

I'm getting close to the end now, and now I'll ask you forgive me for taking liberties that I might not have yet earned.

I know there are things in your past that you don't want to share, and I respect your privacy. I haven't gone snooping. I like to think that if we had more time together, you would have eventually trusted me with some of those secrets, and maybe you would have taken some advice. Since we didn't have that time, I'll ask for some leeway when it comes to telling you something that I wish I would have figured out when I was your age.

Don't be afraid to live the life you've always wanted.

It doesn't matter if that life is being single and running a private investigation firm, or getting married and being a stay-at-home mom. Go back to college or become an apprentice. Make friends or be a loner. Find a man, a woman, or both. The opportunities are endless.

Don't allow fear of your past, or of your future, keep you from reaching that potential.

I swallowed hard, a painful lump in my throat.

Now, for a few final things.

Don't let Wendy Mikelson weasel her way out of payments. She knows that she doesn't get a frequent customer discount. If she has a problem paying the bill, remind her that she can always ask her son to tell her where he's going at all times rather than having us follow him.

Don't take any cases from Hiram Whitehouse. He believes that aliens impregnate his chickens every few months. He's harmless and I don't like taking money from him for his flights of fancy so I just suggest he take any suspicious eggs to his vet. Orville knows all about the alien chickens and doesn't mind turning them into omelets.

When the bathroom sink gets plugged up, before you call a plumber, use the wrench in the tool box to take off the bottom pipe. It'll save you sixty bucks even if it makes you curse.

Go to at least one Rams game and mingle with the locals.

Become a part of the community, even if you're an introverted one.

And, finally, I believe in you, kid. I'm just sorry I won't be around to see everything you're going to accomplish.

Love, Adare

I set the letter back on the desk and rubbed the backs of my hands across my cheeks. I'd always known that life wasn't fair – when your father murdered your mother and two other people, and left you literally scarred for life, the world being *unfair* was sort of a given – but thinking about how my father was still alive while Adare was dead really drove the point home.

I'd wanted to become an FBI agent to make a difference, to protect people the way I hadn't been able to protect my mother. When I'd gotten kicked out of the academy for lying about changing my name and about my father's murder conviction, I'd felt like I'd failed my mother. Becoming a PI hadn't been part of the plan at all. Then the case Jalen had brought me ended up leading to the arrests of several human traffickers and the rescue of several teenage girls. *That* had made a difference.

Maybe I could make my mother proud *and* do what Adare had asked of me and run Burkart Investigations. I'd probably still have to take cases like lost pets or following possibly cheating spouses, but I could find other cases too.

In fact, I realized suddenly, I already knew someone who worked important cases with the FBI even though she wasn't an agent. Jenna Archer. The victim of a childhood horrific enough to make my family look like the Bradys, Jenna was a computer genius and she'd helped FBI agent Raymond Matthews take down several human trafficking and child pornography rings. Oddly enough, Agent Matthews was Clay's partner, both of them working out of the Denver office.

All these pieces of my life had come together in a way that I'd never expected, never could have predicted. If I was someone who believed in destiny or fate, I might've thought that was what was happening here, but I'd seen too much shit to want to believe that there was some higher power or higher reason making things happen.

I preferred to think that the accident that had turned my loving father into a murderous monster had been just that. A serious of circumstances and events, results of choices or of completely happenstance. Why would I want to believe that there had been a reason for my mother being brutally murdered? For Jenna being pimped out by her own mother? For my uncle being shot to death?

I shook my head. Too many maudlin thoughts. I'd come here happier than I'd been since I was a kid, and I wanted that back.

Work. That's what I needed to focus on. Get back to the entire reason I'd come here to begin with. Keeping my promise to Adare.

Even though we'd – *I'd* – been closed for two weeks, I did have a case to work on while I waited for others to come in.

I'd met Jenna on a case. She'd hired me to find the half-brothers and sisters that her mother had given up or had taken from her. I'd gathered some information about them already, but between Adare's hospitalization and death, and then my needing to go back to Indiana for my father's new trial, things had been on hold. Now, it was time to pick them back up again.

Fortunately, my white board was still against the far wall,

turned around to prevent clients from seeing personal information, and everything I'd put on it before was still there.

I walked across the office and turned the board so I could refresh my memory. At the top was Jenna's mother. I'd listed all of the aliases I'd been able to find, including what I knew of which name Jenna's mother used for the different births, and the approximate years each child was born. I still had a lot of blanks to fill, and I intended to work my ass off to give Jenna a chance to know siblings who might end up being a part of her life.

I'd focus on the kids who were born after Helen Kingston's arrest and induction into Witness Protection, mostly because that was the research I could do around here. In another one of those strange twists that I kept seeing, Helen had been sent from Florida to Cheyenne, Wyoming... where she ended up being far too close to Jenna. It was a fuck up of epic proportions on the part of the US Marshals; one that had almost gotten Jenna killed a few years ago.

But, there was one positive to her having been that close. If – no, *when* – I found her siblings, they'd be close enough for them to have a relationship if they wanted it. The older ones would be more difficult to locate, but if there was a way to find them, I'd do it.

I couldn't change what Jenna had been through, but I could do this for her.

End of preview. Played by Him is available now.

ALSO BY M. S. PARKER

His Obsession

His Control

His Hunger

His Secret

Sex Coach

Big O's (Sex Coach 2)

Pleasure Island (Sex Coach 3)

Rescued by the Woodsman

The Billionaire's Muse

Bound

One Night Only

Damage Control

Take Me, Sir

Make Me Yours

The Billionaire's Sub

The Billionaire's Mistress

Con Man Box Set

HERO Box Set

A Legal Affair Box Set

The Client

Indecent Encounter

Dom X Box Set

Unlawful Attraction Box Set

Chasing Perfection Box Set

Blindfold Box Set

Club Prive Box Set

The Pleasure Series Box Set

Exotic Desires Box Set

Casual Encounter Box Set

Sinful Desires Box Set

Twisted Affair Box Set

Serving HIM Box Set

Pure Lust Box Set

ABOUT THE AUTHOR

M. S. Parker is a USA Today Bestselling author and the author of over fifty spicy romance series and novels.

Living part-time in Las Vegas, part-time on Maui, she enjoys sitting by the pool with her laptop writing her next spicy romance.

Growing up all she wanted to be was a dancer, actor and author. So far only the latter has come true but M. S. Parker hasn't retired her dancing shoes just yet. She is still waiting for the call to appear on Dancing With The Stars.

When M. S. isn't writing, she can usually be found reading– oops, scratch that! She is always writing.

For more information:
www.msparker.com
msparkerbooks@gmail.com

ACKNOWLEDGMENTS

First, I would like to thank all of my readers. Without you, my books would not exist. I truly appreciate each and every one of you.

A big THANK YOU goes out to all the Facebook fans, street team, beta readers, and advanced reviewers. You are a HUGE part of the success of all my series.

Also thank you to my editor Lynette, my proofreader Nancy, and my wonderful cover designer, Sinisa. You make my ideas and writing look so good.

36342245R00146

Made in the USA
Middletown, DE
14 February 2019